CW00485238

Storm From Th

Robert Jackson

© Robert Jackson 1974

Robert Jackson has asserted his rights under the Copyright, Design and Patents Act, 1988, to be identified as the author of this work.

First published in 1974 by Arthur Baker Ltd.

This edition published in 2017 by Endeavour Press Ltd.

Table of Contents

1 - The Casablanca Directive

The bitter year of 1942, with all its sacrifices, was over. As the New Year dawned over a world at war, it brought with it the first clear rays of hope that, over the horizon, lay an end to the suffering and misery that had darkened the face of mankind for three long years. At long last the tide of war was beginning to turn in the Allies' favour. In the frozen wastes of Russia the *Wehrmacht*, powerless to intervene, watched the systematic destruction of General Paulus's 6th Army in Stalingrad; in North Africa, following the Allied landings of November 1942 and the British 8th Army's great offensive in the wake of the Battle of Alamein, the remnants of Erwin Rommel's once-proud Afrika Korps were being hounded towards their last battle in Tunisia; in the Atlantic naval hunter-killer groups and long-range aircraft were scoring greater successes against the u-boat wolfpacks that preyed on the Allied convoys; while in the Far East the United States, recovered from the disaster of Pearl Harbour, had fought the Japanese to a standstill and was on the point of hurling its mighty naval task forces across the vastness of the Pacific towards the home islands of Japan.

There was no doubt on either side that 1943 would be the decisive year, the year in which the Allies, as the enemy was well aware, would attempt an invasion of Occupied Europe. Where that blow would fall no one yet knew, not even the Allies themselves, for the policy governing the conduct of the war in Europe at the close of the North African campaign had yet to be determined.

It was for this purpose that a top-level conference between President Roosevelt, Prime Minister Winston Churchill and the Combined Allied Chiefs of Staff was scheduled to take place at the earliest suitable date in 1943. The venue was Casablanca, in French Morocco, and as 1942 drew to a close stringent security precautions were enforced in the town and its environs to ensure that the Allied leaders and their staffs would be safe from enemy attack. In an area as cosmopolitan as this it was too much to hope that the conference would remain a closely guarded secret, and Allied Intelligence was therefore assigned the task of working out every possible method that might be used by the enemy to launch an attack on Casablanca so that appropriate countermeasures could be devised.

On one point Allied Intelligence was certain: there was no possibility of an enemy air attack on Casablanca. The Germans had no long-range bomber force, the nearest *Luftwaffe* air base was over a thousand miles away — beyond the range of medium bombers — and even if a base nearer to Casablanca could have been obtained the *Luftwaffe's* bomber force, which at this stage of the war was on the decline, was in no position to mount a large-scale precision attack.

Allied Intelligence, however, was not entirely correct in its assumptions, as the *Luftwaffe* was soon to prove. In the grey dawn of New Year's morning, 1943, five four-engined Focke-Wulf FW 200 Kondor reconnaissance bombers of Kampfgeschwader 40 took off from their base at Bordeaux, in south-west France, and set course southwards over the Atlantic, skirting the western flank of Spain and Portugal, KG 40 was the one *Luftwaffe* unit Allied Intelligence had overlooked, mainly because its primary role was maritime reconnaissance rather than bombing. Now, entirely on the initiative of its commanding officer — who had simply become bored with a long succession of fruitless twelve-hour patrols over the ocean — KG 40 was on its way to bomb a land target. It was pure coincidence that the German co had selected Casablanca, an attack on which — in view of the numerous Allied headquarters based there since the North African landings — would doubtless serve to shake up the British and Americans. He had no idea how well his scheme would work.

One of the Focke-Wulfs turned back with engine trouble. The others reached the Casablanca area and dropped sixteen 250-kg bombs, achieving complete surprise before escaping out to sea. All four Focke-Wulfs subsequently had to land on Spanish airfields, short of fuel, and the crews who took part — together with KG 40's co — were all severely reprimanded for carrying out the raid without the sanction of higher authority.

The damage inflicted on Casablanca and its surroundings by KG was negligible. Nevertheless the raid showed that the *Luftwaffe* still had a few surprises up its sleeve, and immediate steps were taken to strengthen Casablanca's air defences as an insurance against any repetition. But although lone Focke-Wulf Kondors were occasionally sighted off the

African coast during the days that followed, they made no attempt to strike; and they were the only aircraft that could possibly have carried out such a mission.

In a way it was ironic that the lack of long-range bombers should have prevented the *Luftwaffe* from dealing what might have been a crippling blow to the Allied leadership. For one of the decisions reached at Casablanca was to weld the strategic bombing arms of the Royal Air Force and United States Army Air Force into a single mighty weapon whose task would be, in the words of the resulting directive, 'the progressive destruction and dislocation of the German military, industrial and economic system, and the undermining of the morale of the German people to a point where their capacity for armed resistance is fatally weakened.'

From this general statement of aim the directive went on to be more specific.

Within that general concept [it stated] your primary objectives, subject to the exigencies of weather and of tactical feasibility, will for the present be in the following order of priority:

a. German submarine construction yards.

b. The German aircraft industry.

c. Transportation.

d. Oil plants.

e. Other targets in enemy war industry.

The directive also pointed out that this order of priority was to remain flexible, so that it could be readily altered to meet any changes in the strategic situation. After stressing the need for sustaining attacks on northern Italy and units of the German Navy in harbour, the text of the directive continued:

You should take every opportunity to attack Germany by day, to destroy objectives that are unsuitable for night attack, to sustain continuous pressure on German morale, to impose heavy losses on the German day fighter force and to contain German fighter strength away from the Russian and Mediterranean theatres of war.

Finally, when the Allied armies eventually invaded Europe, the strategic bombing forces were to provide the maximum possible support.

The Casablanca Directive, therefore, was intended as a guideline for the conduct of the Allied strategic bombing offensive up to the ultimate

7

goal of invasion. The overall responsibility for directing the offensive from bases in Great Britain was vested in Marshal of the Royal Air Force Sir Charles Portal, the Chief of Air Staff, although Portal had no authority over the tactics or techniques employed by the United States 8th Air Force. The latter remained under the control of the 8th's commander Lieutenant-General Ira Eaker.

Many senior British and American commanders believed that the terms of the directive were far less specific than they might have been. As it was, a great deal was left to individual interpretation, and in this respect the views of the two Allied bomber commanders in the field — Sir Arthur Harris and General Eaker — differed considerably. As far as Harris was concerned, the key sentence in the directive was 'undermining the morale of the German people', which, he believed, could best be achieved by continuing the massive area attacks on German cities begun by RAF Bomber Command the year before. Eaker, on the other hand, advocated long-range precision attacks on German industrial targets-but since the 8th Air Force had yet to penetrate Germany, the RAF commanders were sceptical about the Americans' ability to carry out a successful daylight offensive at all.

Individual opinions aside, the fact remained that at the beginning of 1943 neither Bomber Command nor the 8th Air Force was in a position to implement the kind of massive strategic offensive envisaged by the Casablanca Directive. Bomber Command's most powerful striking force at the turn of the year was No. 5 Group, with nine squadrons of Lancasters. Apart from that, the Command's available heavy bomber force consisted of only about a hundred Halifaxes and fifty Stirlings. A large number of twin-engined Wellington medium bombers remained in service with the squadrons of Nos 1, 3 and 4 Groups, but in January 1943 many of these were temporarily non-operational pending the formation of eight new squadrons. The latter were to be transferred to the newly-formed No. 6 (Royal Canadian Air Force) Group, which reached operational status on 1 January and was allocated seven bases in Yorkshire. No. 6 Group flew its first mission on the night of 3/4 January 1943, when six Wellingtons of No. 427 Squadron — operating from Croft, near Darlington — laid mines off the Frisian Islands.

The shortage of long-range heavy bombers made itself felt during the early weeks of 1943, when the brunt of Bomber Command's strategic offensive had to be borne by No. 5 Group. In particular it had an adverse effect on long-standing plans to carry out a large-scale attack on Berlin, a target which — although it had been high on the list of Bomber Command's priorities during 1942 — had not been attacked at all in the course of that year. The main reason was that the small force of bombers which Bomber Command would have been able to put up against the German capital on any one occasion during 1942 would not have been able to achieve significant damage, and would in all probability have suffered heavy losses during the long four-hour flight over strongly-defended areas of enemy territory.

Towards the end of 1942, however, the demand for an attack on Berlin became more urgent, and with the availability of No. 5 Group's Lancaster squadrons in strength the project at last became feasible. It was accordingly decided to attack Berlin as early as possible in January, in conjunction with a diversionary attack on a target close to Berlin by a force of Halifaxes and Stirlings. At no time during the first two weeks of January, however, were sufficient Halifaxes and Stirlings available to undertake this task, with the result that No. 5 Group's Lancasters had to carry out the raid unsupported on the night of 16/17 January. The target marking, carried out by aircraft of the Pathfinder Force, was not very precise, and the bombing was consequently scattered. Nevertheless damage was inflicted on several factories in the suburbs of Berlin, and only one aircraft was lost out of the entire attacking force. It was a different story the following night, when the Lancasters again attacked the enemy capital. This time there was no cloud cover, and in the brilliant moonlight the enemy night-fighters found no difficulty in locating their targets. Twenty-two bombers failed to return.

Meanwhile the Americans were making plans to go ahead with their own strategic offensive against Germany. The United States long-range bomber force, equipped with B-17 Flying Fortresses and B-24 Liberators, had been building up steadily on bases in East Anglia since the spring of 1942. The first American bombing attack from Britain, with fighter cover provided by the Spitfire squadrons of No. 11 Group, RAF, took place on 17 August 1942 against the marshalling yards at Rouen. The bombing, carried out in good weather conditions, achieved excellent results, and during the rest of the year the American daylight bombers carried out many more successful attacks on targets in France and the

Low Countries, all of them within range of fighter escort. American plans to attack targets in Germany were delayed for a variety of reasons, mainly the lack of fighter escort and the Allied landings in North Africa, which helped to set back the 8th Air Force's buildup in Britain because of the pressing need for heavy bombers in the Mediterranean theatre. But by the beginning of January 1943 General Eaker had 500 B-17s under his command and he judged that the time was ripe for the big daylight offensive to begin.

The Americans believed that they could best fulfil the demands of the Casablanca Directive by carrying out concentrated daylight attacks on six principal target systems, designed to achieve the maximum destruction in selected major industries. These systems were, in order of priority, submarine construction yards and bases, the aircraft industry, the ball-bearing industry, oil production, synthetic rubber production and factories producing military transport.

The target selected for the first American raid on Germany was one that fell into the leading category of objectives: the big naval base at Wilhelmshaven, a major centre of u-boat production. During the last week of January air reconnaissance revealed that the production yards were in full swing and that, as an added bonus, the pocket battleship *Admiral Scheer* was in dry dock on the north side of the Bauhafen.

On the morning of 27 January fifty-five B-17s took off from their English bases and set course over the North Sea. The weather was far from ideal for high-level precision bombing, and at altitude the cold was intense. The sub-zero temperatures knifed through the thickest flying clothing; machine-guns, turrets and camera mechanisms froze solid, while windscreens and bomb sights were obscured by opaque layers of frost. One of the navigators described the outward flight:

At about 10.30 the altimeter indicated 25,000 feet. The cloud cover had ended, far below us, and we could see the surface of the sea — like a sheet of glass. At 10.45 the Captain warned the crew to be extra alert. I looked out to the right and could see the outline of the coast of Germany and the row of islands that lay just off it. At 10.57 we were just over the islands and at 11.00 the tail gunner reported flak at six o'clock, below. It was from the coastal islands and was the first time we were fired on from German soil. At this time we were beginning to turn and we crossed the island of Baltrum and went into German territory. As we turned, the bombardier elevated the muzzle of his gun and fired a burst so that the tracers arched over into Germany. The first shots from our ship, 'Hell's Angel', but not the last!

The American raid took the German defences by surprise. Fifty-three Fortresses unloaded their bombs on the Wilhelmshaven harbour installations, opposed by only a handful of Focke-Wulf 190s of *Jagdgeschwader* 1, led by Lieutenant-Colonel Erich Mix; two more Fortresses bombed Emden. Only three B-17S failed to return, appearing to vindicate the Americans' belief that fears for the success of long-range daylight operations were unfounded. They were to be proven tragically wrong, but that was still in the future.

Meanwhile RAF Bomber Command was planning a long-range daylight raid of its own — a masterly surprise attack of the type that was to characterize its operations throughout the war. From Intelligence sources it was established that a big military parade was to be held in Berlin on 30 January, to mark the formation of the German Army ten years earlier. In addition a radio broadcast to the German people was to be made at 11.00 by Reichs-marschall Hermann Göring, followed by a second broadcast at 16.00 by the propaganda minister Goebbels.

Disrupting the proceedings of the big day would be no easy task; at this stage of the war no Allied aircraft had yet ventured over Berlin in daylight. Nevertheless the Bomber Command planning staff was confident that one RAF bomber type could carry out the mission and get away safely — the twin-engined de Havil-land Mosquito. In January 1943 two squadrons in No. 2 Group -Nos 105 and 139-were equipped with these versatile machines, and on the 27th both these units carried out a daylight raid on the shipbuilding yards of Burmeister and Wain at Copenhagen. Nine aircraft took part led by Wing Commander Hughie Edwards. The Mosquitoes swept over the Danish capital at between 50 and 300 feet, heading for the island to the east of the city where the shipbuilding yards were sited. The aircraft ran the gauntlet of intense flak from shore batteries and ships in the harbour and two were shot down. The remainder bombed the target successfully and returned to base after a 1,400-mile round trip lasting five hours and thirteen minutes.

Three days later the Mosquitoes were detailed to undertake their most dangerous mission so far. At 08.45 three aircraft of No. 105 Squadron, led by Squadron Leader R. W. Reynolds, took off from Marham in

Norfolk and set course out over the North Sea. The plan called for them to drop their bombs on Berlin at exactly 11.00, to coincide with the start of Göring's radio speech, and this called for some highly precise work on the part of Reynolds' navigator Pilot Officer E. B. Sismore.

The morning was brilliantly clear. The Mosquitoes crossed the North Sea at low level, then began to climb hard as they entered German territory. A few minutes before 11 o'clock the lakes around Berlin showed up as metallic patches, glistening in the sunshine. The bombers made their runs across the city through only scattered flak — there were no enemy fighters — and released their 500-pounders exactly on schedule.

In Britain German linguists monitoring the German Radio shortly before 11.00 heard the announcer tell the audience to stand by for an important speech by Göring. Then, at 11.00 to the second, the announcer's voice was punctuated by the plainly-heard sound of exploding bombs and the programme faded out, to be replaced by martial music. It was thirty minutes before Göring finally came on the air, and the tone of his voice left the listeners in no doubt that he was plainly harrassed and angry. By that time the three Mosquitoes were safely on their way home.

At 13.25 three more Mosquitoes, this time drawn from No. 139 Squadron and led by Squadron Leader D. F. W. Darling, also took off from Marham. They flew at wave-top height to a point north of Heligoland, then turned in towards Lübeck. By this time the weather had deteriorated, and the aircraft ran through squalls along the whole of their route. The German defences too were on the alert, as the attackers soon discovered. As the Mosquitoes climbed up to 20,000 feet Sergeant R. C. Fletcher, the navigator in the number two aircraft, shouted a warning: Messerschmitt 109s were attacking from astern.

Fletcher's pilot Sergeant J. Massey, and Flight Sergeant P. J. McGeehan flying the number three aircraft, both took violent evasive action and managed to shake off the fighters. Squadron Leader Darling was not so lucky. He was last seen diving down into cloud, apparently out of control, and failed to return from the mission.

The two remaining Mosquitoes flew on above a dense cloud layer. At 15.55 they arrived over Berlin and Sergeant Massey dropped his bombs through a gap in the clouds. By this time the flak was intense, and it was another eight minutes before Flight Sergeant McGeehan could get into position to make a successful bombing run. His bombs burst about half a mile south of the city centre. As the Mosquitoes turned for home Goebbels' speech went out as planned — from an underground radio station. Their noses down to gain speed, the two bombers raced for the coast, evading the worst of the flak and several Focke-Wulf 190s that tried to intercept them. They landed at Marham at 18.30, having proved that from now on the inhabitants of Berlin could expect no respite from the Allied bombs even in daylight.

While the long-range bomber squadrons of the RAF and USAAF probed into Germany with growing confidence during January and February 1943, much of the Allied bombing effort during these freezing winter weeks was devoted to minelaying and attacks on enemy-held naval bases in France, with u-boat pens receiving top priority. The record of No. 419 (Moose) Squadron -one of the units in the newly-formed No. 6 (RCAF) Group-during this period was fairly typical. Flying Halifaxes from Middleton-St-George, near Darlington, No. 419 carried out twenty-one operational missions in January and February. Of these eleven were minelaying missions and the rest were bombing attacks on the enemy submarine bases of Lorient, Wilhelmshaven, Hamburg and St Nazaire.

The squadron sustained crew losses on three occasions, twice while engaged in laying mines off the Frisian Islands. Two members of a third crew were also killed, and a fourth aircraft was lost through ditching. The fatal casualties occurred aboard a Halifax captained by Sergeant John McIntosh, the bomber having been severely damaged by fire from a flak ship and the cannon of an enemy night-fighter. The flight engineer and the rear gunner were killed, and the navigator, Sergeant Art Mellin, was hit in the leg, suffering a compound fracture. Despite the severity of his wounds and their crippling effect, Mellin temporarily assumed the duties of the dead engineer while other members of the crew fought to put out a fire in the fuselage. Mellin later resumed his navigation, plotting courses that brought the aircraft safely back to England and enabled the pilot to make an emergency landing on Coltishall airfield. Although he had lost a lot of blood and was in extreme pain, Mellin insisted on remaining at his post until the airfield was in sight. His courage was subsequently recognized by the award of the Distinguished Flying Medal.

The Halifax that ditched had already made one minelaying run off the Frisians and was about to make another when multiple engine trouble, caused by unsuspected flak damage, developed to a point where the bomber could no longer maintain flying speed without losing height. The ditching procedure, from the touchdown to the boarding of the dinghy, was accomplished without trouble. The crew were picked up late the following day, having suffered no ill effects despite drifting for twenty-two hours in the icy North Sea.

Towards the end of February 1943, as Bomber Command geared up its resources for the great offensive that was to come, the tempo of air operations increased considerably. For the squadrons in No. 6 Group, the night of 1 March marked the first mission against Berlin, and for many crews it was a harrowing experience. The weather was good; for once atmospheric conditions were so favourabe that the crews were able to pinpoint their way to the target and release their bombs visually. Geographical features such as the Havel and Spree rivers permitted absolute identification, and fires concentrated around the aiming point were reflected as countless flickering lights in the waters of the Havel See, their glow visible from 150 miles away. However the flak was intense, and several crews had narrow escapes. One of the luckiest escapes of all was experienced by Sergeant J. N. Thompson, a 419 Squadron rear gunner. As he was searching the sky for fighters on his way in to the target, a flak burst neatly removed the door of his turret from its hinges. He himself was unharmed, but he completed the rest of the trip frozen stiff.

Forty-eight hours later the target was Hamburg, which was attacked in the teeth of fierce opposition. Then, on 4 March, an electrifying rumour spread through Bomber Command to the effect that a major bombing offensive was about to begin. The rumour was true. On the night of 5/6 March a large force of RAF bombers took off to attack Essen. The martyrdom of the Ruhr and of the major German cities extending over the fatherland towards Berlin was starting.

2 - RAF Night Bombing Operations, 1943-4

At 20.50 hours in the evening of 5 March 1943 a lone Mosquito of No. 109 Squadron droned high over darkened Germany. Ahead lay the sprawling complex of the Ruhr and the town of Essen, with searchlight beams playing through the industrial haze and sporadic anti-aircraft fire flickering across the sky.

At 21.00 precisely the Mosquito crew, bombing blindly with the aid of 'Oboe', released a cluster of red target indicators (TIS); these burst close to the aiming point, the big Krupps armament factory. Two minutes later a salvo of green TIS also burst nearby; these were dropped by a Lancaster of the Pathfinder Force (PFF), sighting on the original group of TIS. At 21.03 a second 109 Squadron Mosquito, also bombing with the help of Oboe, dropped a salvo of TIS in turn, followed by another PFF Lancaster with green markers. The process continued until 21.38, with eight 109 Squadron Mosquitoes releasing their markers singly at intervals, backed up by twenty-two heavy bombers of the PFF.

Seven minutes after the first cluster of markers went down the leading heavy bombers of the main force roared over the target. The first wave, consisting of Halifaxes, was scheduled to complete its attack by 21.20; the second, consisting of Stirlings and Wellingtons, between 21.15 and 21.25; and the third, composed of Lancasters, between 21.20 and 21.40. Each wave consequently overlapped the other, and accurate timing was of vital importance. To assist the navigation of the main force, yellow markers were dropped by PFF on track fifteen miles short of the target. Crews were briefed to aim their loads at the red TIS, or the green TIS if the former could not be seen.

Although three of the 109 Squadron Mosquitoes were unable to release their TIS because of the failure of their Oboe equipment, the remaining indicators illuminated the target to such an extent that the main force had no difficulty in locating it. Four Halifax crews in the first wave, bombing two minutes early, inadvertently acted as additional pathfinders. Their bombs, falling squarely in the target area, started several large fires which the 71 Halifax crews that followed were easily able to distinguish.

All the latter aircraft attacked within their specified period, as did 106 of the Wellingtons and Stirlings that formed the second wave; the remaining 35 bombed between two and five minutes early. Of the Lancasters in the final wave 86 also attacked on schedule, the other 43 bombing just outside the time limit.

In all 345 crews claimed to have attacked the target, although later reconnaissance showed that about twenty-five per cent of the bombs had in fact fallen outside the target area. Fifty-six other bombers which took off on the raid failed to reach the target area; forty-eight of these sorties had to be aborted through technical malfunctions, and the other eight included a mid-air collision between two Wellingtons — both of which landed safely — a crash on take-off, damage by a night-fighter, the sickness of a crew and the failure of one crew member to take an oxygen tube. Losses attributed to the enemy included 14 aircraft destroyed and 32 damaged, 27 by flak and 5 by night-fighters.

From night photographs brought back by the main force aircraft it was estimated that at least 153 crews had dropped their bombs within three miles of the aiming point — by far the most accurate result of any attack on Essen so far. Returning crews reported seeing large explosions, together with fires raging over considerable areas, and those in the final wave indicated that the entire target area was obscured by a vast pall of smoke. The general impression was one of great destruction, and this was confirmed by three daylight reconnaissance sorties flown by Photo Reconaissance Spitfires on 7-8 March. Their photographs, which covered the whole of the town with the exception of the north-west, revealed that a 160-acre area of Essen had been completely levelled, and in a further area of 450 acres more than

threequarters of the buildings had been destroyed or severely damaged by high-explosive or incendiary bombs. The Krupp factories had been badly devastated, mainly by fire, with thirteen of their main workshops destroyed or heavily damaged and a further fifty-three buildings damaged to a lesser degree.

So ended Bomber Command's first major operation in the Battle of the Ruhr — an operation noteworthy for the fact that the target had been marked and bombed without actual visual identification. The unparalleled accuracy of the attack, and the devastation it had caused in a relatively confined area, came as a severe shock to both the population of Essen and the German leadership.

The second major raid was carried out on the night of 8/9 March, and this time the target was Nuremberg. Since Nuremberg was well outside the range of the Oboe ground stations in the UK the plan called for a precision attack to be made with the aid of H2S. The initial target marking was to be carried out by five aircraft equipped with this device, which were to drop sticks of flares across the target a few minutes before zero hour. If the objective could be identified visually by the light of the flares, the five aircraft were then to drop green target indicators on it. Two minutes later the process was to be repeated by nine more H2S-equipped aircraft. Meanwhile twenty-one bombers were to attack at one-minute intervals to maintain the marking, dropping their mixed loads of high explosive and incendiary on the aiming point, if the latter could be identified, and on the centre of the concentration of green TIS if it could not. If neither the target nor the green TIS could be seen, the bombers were to release red TIS with the aid of H2S.

As in the Essen raid, the main force was to attack in three overlapping waves. Eighty-eight Halifaxes in the first wave were to bomb from zero plus four until zero plus fifteen, 53 Stirlings in the second wave from zero plus ten to zero plus twenty, and 157 Lancasters in the final wave from zero plus fifteen to zero plus thirty. All the main-force crews were briefed to disregard all visual ground details and aim their bombs at the centre of the target indicators.

The fourteen H2S-equipped marker aircraft arrived over the target on schedule, but because of extensive ground haze their crews found difficulty in locating the precise aiming point. Nine of the aircraft released their markers blindly, with the aid of H2S; the others released visually, but only because their equipment went unserviceable at the last moment. The overall result was that the target indicators were widely scattered, covering an area between seven miles south and two miles north-west of the aiming point.

Nevertheless of the 294 main force crews who claimed to have attacked the target, 142 dropped their bombs within three miles of the aiming point, and the damage inflicted — although not as concentrated as that in the Essen raid — was substantial. Daylight reconnaissance showed that industrial areas in the southern sector of the city had suffered heavily. The Siemens factory was two-thirds destroyed, and large areas of the M.A.N. works-which produced diesel engines for the German u-boat fleet-had been completely wrecked. Bomber Command's loss during this operation was exceptionally light: seven aircraft failed to return and fifteen suffered varying degrees of damage.

One of the main conclusions drawn from the results of these two attacks was that the most widespread damage was likely to result from a heavy concentration of incendiary bombs. Future raids on German cities should, therefore, be centred on the most inflammable part of the target area to ensure the rapid spreading of the conflagration, and the most inflammable sector was usually the centre of the city rather than the suburbs, where buildings were of more modern and durable construction.

On the night of 12/13 March Essen was once again the target, the attack following much the same pattern as the previous one. Three hundred and eighty-four main-force bombers hit the target in the wake of the Oboe-equipped Mosquitoes, and subsequent daylight reconnaissance photos showed that the Krupp factory had once again been badly hit and that heavy damage had been inflicted on the north-west suburbs. On this occasion, however, Bomber Command also suffered: 23 bombers failed to return and 69 were damaged. Ten of the missing bombers were apparently shot down by night fighters and ten by flak.

The third major attack on Essen was carried out on the night of 3/4 April, with 348 aircraft despatched. Because the weather forecast suggested cloud over the target at various levels the Oboe Mosquito crews were briefed to drop both ground and sky markers. This was done on schedule but led to some confusion among the main-force crews, who had not been briefed to expect sky markers. This, however, did not detract from the success of the operation: 172 of the bombers dropped their loads within three miles of the aiming point, and once again the devastation was considerable. Each of the Halifaxes taking part in the raid carried two 1,000-pound bombs and incendiaries; the Lancasters of 5 Group carried 4,000-pounders plus incendiaries with the exception of six aircraft which were laden with 8,000-pounders. Twenty-one aircraft failed to return and fifty-nine were damaged, amounting to twenty-three per cent of the attacking force. Returning bomber crews reported intense night-fighter activity over the target, the German crews braving intense flak to reach the bomber stream. Two of the night's losses, however, were Halifaxes which crashed on landing at their home bases.

The fourth raid on Essen, on the night of 30 April/1 May, was marred by dense cloud, and on this occasion the Mosquitoes were briefed to drop sky markers at five-minute intervals during the attack, which was scheduled to begin at 02.30. The sky markers were to precede each new wave of bombers, whose run-in to the target was to be further assisted by flares dropped by the Mosquitoes on the approaches. Two marker Mosquitoes were held in reserve and these should have been called in when, for technical reasons, the last of the Pathfinder Mosquitoes was unable to drop its markers. They failed to go into action, however, with the result that when the final wave of main-force bombers started their run to the target no markers were visible. The crews in the third wave were consequently forced to release their bombs by reference to a datum point which they had been given during their briefing.

In all 239 crews claimed to have attacked Essen; 3 reported bombing alternative targets, 51 aborted and 12 failed to return. Forty-five other aircraft were damaged, all but three by antiaircraft fire. Although the Krupp factory was once again hit, no new damage appeared to have been caused.

The sky-marking technique was also used on the fifth massive attack on Essen, carried out on the night of 27/28 May by 518 aircraft. This time the marker force was increased to ten Mosquitoes, which were scheduled to drop their sky markers at five-minute intervals beginning at 00.45 and ending at 01.30. Once again one of the Mosquitoes was unable to release its markers owing to technical trouble, but this time the gap was filled by the two reserves, and 472 aircraft of the main force successfully located the target, aiming their bombs at the sky markers or at the position of those seen to go out. Twenty-two aircraft, including one of the marker Mosquitoes, failed to return and 113 were damaged by enemy action. Five others were accidentally damaged, one when it was hit by incendiary bombs from an aircraft higher up, two more when they were hit by machine-gun fire from other bombers, and the remaining two — a Halifax and a Lancaster-as the result of a mid-air collision. Direct hits were once again obtained on the area of the Krupp factory, but this raid and the one before it proved conclusively that, in terms of results, sky markers were greatly inferior to ground target indicators. In all,

Bomber Command despatched 2,070 sorties to Essen in the course of these five attacks, at a cost of 92 aircraft which failed to return and 334 damaged.

The sky-marking technique, meanwhile, had also been used extensively in Bomber Command's offensive against Duisburg, which was attacked more frequently than any other target during the Battle of the Ruhr. The first three attacks in March and April, carried out with sky markers, produced little result. A total of 955 aircraft were despatched, but they failed to achieve any real bombing concentration. Thirty-three aircraft failed to return from these missions and seventy-six more were damaged.

The fourth attack, carried out on the night of 26/27 April, was also a failure, even though on this occasion the main force was preceded by 6 Oboe-equipped Mosquitoes which dropped red TIS, and throughout the attack green TIS were released at regular intervals by 26 backup aircraft. Reconnaissance later showed that about 150 aircraft had succeeded in placing their bombs within three miles of the aiming point but that the actual damage inflicted on Duisburg was surprisingly light, probably because the town was a relatively small target with large open spaces between its built-up areas. The final attack, however, made on the night of 12/13 May, went off extremely well. Nine Oboe Mosquitoes succeeded in placing their TIS within two miles of the aiming point, and these — together with other indicators dropped by the backup force — enabled a large proportion of the 572 main-force aircraft despatched to achieve a good bombing concentration. It was estimated in fact that no fewer than 410 crews had managed to drop their loads within three miles of the aiming point, causing almost complete devastation over a 48-acre area of the old town. Substantial damage was also caused in the suburbs, where several factories — including four belonging to the Thyssen steel group — had been severely hit.

This last attack showed that ground marking was generally the most effective means of achieving results if the weather permitted, and this was substantiated by the results of other attacks carried out during the Battle of the Ruhr. On the nights of 4 and 23 May massive damage was inflicted on Dortmund in the course of two highly concentrated Oboe-directed attacks. A similar raid on Dusseldorf on the night of 25/26 May failed because of dense cloud, but the town was revisited on the night of

11 /12 June and its centre shattered. On the next night Bomber Command attacked Bochum and destroyed 130 acres of the town's heart, and on 25/26 July an Oboe attack on Aachen resulted in the destruction of more than half the town's area.

One of the most effective Oboe-directed attacks of all, however, took place on the night of 29/30 May against the Barmen district of Wuppertal. Of the 719 aircraft despatched 611 claimed to have attacked the target; 62 aborted, 33 failed to return and 71 were damaged, but reconnaissance showed that at least 475 crews had dropped their bombs within three miles of the aiming point. This in itself was no mean achievement, as the Oboe Mosquitoes' timing was very poor throughout the attack: the initial batch of markers went down only two minutes late, but then there was a gap of eighteen minutes before the second batch. The situation was probably saved by the first Mosquito, which dropped its indicators with extreme accuracy, and most of the green TIS released by the twelve backup aircraft — together with a great many incendiaries dropped by the first wave of the main force — fell in this immediate area. The heavy concentration of markers completely overwhelmed any attempt by the Germans to confuse the main force by igniting decoy flares, and more than compensated for the initial delay. Because of this concentration, the bombing wrought havoc over an area of a thousand acres, with ninety per cent of the built-up areas in the suburbs wrecked and half the remainder of the town damaged to a more or less severe degree. From daylight reconnaissance photographs it was estimated that 34,000 dwelling houses had been made uninhabitable, and that at least 118,000 people had been made homeless. The main railway station was immobilized, as were two electric power stations, the gasworks and the waterworks. In addition hits had been obtained on five vital factories and 108 other industrial establishments.

This attack was followed, on the night of 14/15 June, by a smaller but equally devastating raid on Oberhausen, which was carried out in cloudy conditions aided by sky-marking techniques. Two hundred and three aircraft were despatched and 146 crews claimed to have attacked the target, although because of the heavy cloud no accurate analysis could be made from the night photographs the returning aircraft brought back. The next day, however, photo-reconnaissance showed that the centre of Oberhausen had been virtually levelled.

Although the success achieved in these attacks on targets in the Ruhr Valley generally surpassed Bomber Command's expectations, it was a different story when the Command launched heavy area attacks on other German targets which lay outside the range of Oboe. An attack on Munich early in March caused only light damage, while another on Stuttgart on the night of the nth/12th failed almost completely. Towards the end of the month two raids were made on Berlin, and out of nearly 500 aircraft that took part only 3 appeared to have dropped their bombs within three miles of the aiming point; a further 281 missed it by more than five miles. At the beginning of April 577 aircraft attacked Kiel, and again only relatively light damage was caused. No bombing concentration whatsoever was achieved during a raid on Frankfurt on the night of 10/n April, and although the bombers inflicted substantial damage on the suburbs of Stuttgart during a second attack on the night of 14/15 April, only a handful fell near the aiming point, which lay at the centre of the town.

A mission against the big Skoda armaments factory at Pilsen on the night of 16/17 April produced the same negative result, but the main contributory factor here was that the Pathfinders mistook a large mental hospital near Dobrany for the factory and placed their TIS squarely on it. As a result, although 249 crews claimed to have attacked the target, subsequent reconnaissance showed that only 6 crews had in fact placed their bombs within three miles of it. An excellent concentration was achieved during a second attack on Pilsen on the night of 13/14 May, but unfortunately the concentration occurred in open fields two miles north of the Skoda works.

There were, of course, exceptions to this depressing pattern of poor results. On the night of 20/21 April a major raid was mounted against Stettin, and out of the 304 crews who claimed to have attacked the target 256 succeeded in placing their bombs within three miles of the aiming point, devastating about a hundred acres of industrial sites. Another highly successful long-range attack was carried out on the night of 11/12 June against Münster. Seventy-two aircraft of the Pathfinder Force were despatched and 60 crews claimed to have attacked. Forty-three sticks of bombs fell close to the aiming point, and a PR Mosquito that flew over the area the following day reported that the centre of the town appeared to have suffered heavily and was still burning.

Although some of the long-range failures were due to the malfunctioning of target markers and poor timing on the part of the main force, which sometimes arrived over the target to find that the TIS had gone out, the overriding reason was the limitation of H2S, which was used on all the long-distance attacks. The original plan had been to use H2S only for dropping flares, in the light of which the ground markers were to have been aimed visually, but because of adverse weather and the height at which the bombers were compelled to fly to escape the worst of the German defences, visual identification of the target was often impossible. Moreover accurate interpretation of H2S was often extremely difficult unless the target was adjacent to some prominent terrain feature such as a river or coastline.

One such target was Hamburg, a city which, during the last week of July and the first week of August, was to receive the full weight of Bomber Command's striking power as the RAF extended its major bombing operations from the Ruhr along the road to Berlin.

The first major attack on Hamburg, carried out on the night of 24/25 July, was noteworthy because it marked the first operational use by Bomber Command of 'Window', strips of tinfoil cut to the wavelength of the German radar. Although Window had been perfected early in 1942, the decision to use it operationally had been postponed in case the Germans also developed it for use by the *Luftwaffe's* bomber force. It was only in March 1943, when it was finally realized that the German bomber arm no longer presented a serious threat to the British Isles, that the situation took a new turn. Bomber Command's losses were increasing all the time, and it was estimated that about seventy per cent of the total casualties were due to enemy night-fighter activity. Since the enemy night fighters were radar controlled they were susceptible to radar jamming, as were a large number of anti-aircraft batteries, and consequently the Air Staff estimated that it might be possible to cut down the Command's loss rate by something like thirty-five per cent. Even then the decision to employ Window was subjected to still more delay, primarily because it was feared that if the Germans began using it on a large scale they might seriously interfere with Allied plans for the invasion of Sicily, scheduled for the summer of 1943.

Meanwhile, as the Air Staff wavered, Bomber Command lost 858 aircraft between 1 April and the middle of July 1943. It was not until 15

July that the Cabinet gave the necessary approval for the introduction of Window, and the date of its operational debut was fixed for the 23rd. The following night 791 heavy bombers, comprising 347 Lancasters, 246 Halifaxes, 125 Stirlings and 73 Wellingtons, set course for Hamburg, flying a wide detour over the North Sea and turning in to make landfall on the German coast near the Elbe Estuary. Ahead of the main force 6 aircraft equipped with H2S dropped yellow markers over the crossing point on the coast, at the same time transmitting their estimate of the latest wind conditions to a ground station in the UK for relay to the other bombers.

The whole force was scheduled to start dropping Window on reaching longitude 7 degrees 30 minutes east, and was to carry on doing so until it passed 7 degrees east on the outward journey. The attack was timed to begin at 00.57 with the dropping of yellow TIS and flares over Hamburg by 20 H2S-equipped aircraft. This was to permit the crews of 8 more H2S aircraft to identify the target visually and mark the aiming point at the centre of the city with red TIS. Fifty-three backup aircraft were also to drop green TIS between zero plus two and zero plus forty-eight, aiming primarily at the red markers. The main-force attack was scheduled to start at zero plus two and was to last for forty-eight minutes. The main-force crews were briefed to aim at the red TIS or, if these could not be seen, at the centre of the concentration of green markers.

The attack opened on schedule. Most of the green markers landed near the centre of the target area, but the red TIS were widely scattered and grouped around four separate points. However although the bombing tended to concentrate around these points at first, the backup aircraft helped to keep the assault reasonably well centred throughout the raid, and 306 out of the 728 crews who claimed to have attacked the target dropped their bombs within three miles of the aiming point. But a considerable creep-back developed as the raid progressed, and by 01.30 a trail of incendiaries stretched over a distance of seven miles on the approach to the city.

Twelve aircraft failed to return from this mission and 31 were damaged, the casualties being inflicted by flak and night-fighters in roughly equal proportions. The damaged aircraft included two Lancasters which collided over the UK. Another Lancaster and two Halifaxes were hit by bombs dropped from above, and a fourth Lancaster was damaged when its marker bomb was apparently hit by a flak shell a split second after release. The exceptionally low loss rate was due in the main to the effect of Window, which threw the enemy defences into complete confusion. Forty-six more bombers aborted for various reasons, and five attacked alternative targets. About 1,500 people were killed in the course of the attack, and although on this occasion Hamburg did not suffer substantially more damage than that inflicted earlier on towns in the Ruhr Valley, the raid was judged to have been a success and plans were laid for the onslaught to continue.

On 25 and 26 July the United States 8th Air Force joined the assault, with 235 Fortresses and Liberators bombing the city by daylight. After each of these daylight attacks a small force of Bomber Command Mosquitoes flew nuisance raids against the city, keeping the defences in a state of constant alert and permitting the inhabitants little respite.

Bomber Command's second major operation in the Battle of Hamburg took place on the night of 27/28 July, when a force of 787 Lancasters, Halifaxes, Wellingtons and Stirlings was despatched. This time, instead of routing out over the sea, the bombers flew across the neck of the Danish peninsula and approached Hamburg on a track between Lübeck and the Elbe. The marking tactics were also altered: this time, because of the poor results achieved by the markers in the earlier raid, visual marking was to be abandoned and the markers were to be dropped blindly by 25 crews with the aid of H2S. Window was once again to be dropped during the attack, which was timed to begin at 01.00 and which was to last for forty-three minutes.

The attack opened a little early, and by 01.00 fifteen salvoes of yellow TIS had already been dropped. These were placed with a high degree of accuracy in the Billwärder district, between one-and-a-half and three miles east-south-east of the aiming point. Six hundred and fifty-three crews of the main force consequently found little difficulty in locating the aiming point, and 325 of them dropped their bombs within three miles of it. This time there was little creep-back during the attack and the bombers achieved an impressive concentration of high explosives and incendiaries. The loss rate, thanks to Window, was once again low: 17 of the bombers failed to return and 49 were damaged. The following night the usual small force of Mosquitoes that attacked the city reported that Hamburg was still burning.

The third great blow against the shattered port was struck on the night of 29/30 July. A total of 777 bombers were despatched, but this time the marking was not so accurate and the bombing was widely dispersed. In all, 699 crews claimed to have hit the target, but only 238 appeared to have placed their bombs within the three-mile radius around the aiming point. This time 30 bombers failed to return and 43 were damaged, an indication that Window was beginning to lose some of its effectiveness. Instead of attempting to vector fighters on to individual bombers, the German controllers were now adopting a technique of loose fighter control which involved passing information on the height, course and speed of the main bomber stream to the night-fighter crews and leaving them to work out their own methods of interception.

Nevertheless the combined weight of the three attacks had wrought fearful havoc in Hamburg, and on the night of 2/3 August 740 bombers were sent out to deal the final blow. This operation was the most difficult of all to carry out; weather conditions were distinctly unfavourable, with cumulo-nimbus clouds towering to 25,000 feet on the approaches to Hamburg and the area blanketed by thunderstorms. The cloud over the target was unbroken, extending to 15,000 feet with occasional pillars climbing to as high as 30,000; below it Hamburg was shrouded in torrential rain. Hardly any of the ground markers were visible, and in fact half the main force failed to reach the target. Once again 30 bombers failed to return, and 51 were damaged. Despite the difficulties, however, those aircraft that did get through inflicted still more severe damage.

The overall result of the Battle of Hamburg was encouraging. In four missions Bomber Command had despatched 3,095 sorties. Nine thousand tons of bombs, half of them incendiaries, had gone down on the reeling city, and yet only 86 bombers — amounting to 2.8 per cent of the force sent out-had failed to return. Another 174 had been damaged, making the Command's total casualty rate during the battle 8.4 per cent-less than half that sustained during the five big raids on Essen.

Encouraging though the offensive against Hamburg may have been, however, its success was no ground for over-optimism. The city was an excellent H2S target, and there was no guarantee that a similar success would be registered against other targets along the road to Berlin, especially against Berlin itself. Neither was there any guarantee that, as Window lost its effectiveness, Bomber Command would be able to continue to concentrate its offensive against single targets in this fashion without suffering crippling losses.

Meanwhile towards the end of July two more highly effective Oboe-directed attacks had been made against targets in the Ruhr valley. The first, on the night of 25/26 July, was against Essen.

Eleven Oboe-equipped Mosquitoes released their ground markers with a high degree of accuracy and 604 crews claimed to have attacked the target. Subsequent reconnaissance showed that 368 salvoes of bombs had dropped within three miles of the aiming point. Firestorms swept through the town, and large areas of it burned for several days, causing more damage to Essen than all the previous attacks put together. Vast damage was inflicted on the Krupp works, no of the 190 workshops being destroyed or damaged. In his diary for 28 July Dr Goebbels, the German propaganda minister, recorded that 'the last raid on Essen caused a complete stoppage of production in the Krupps works. Speer is much concerned and worried.'

On the morning after the raid Dr Gustav Krupp von Bohlen und Halbach came down to his office, surveyed the twisted wreckage of his factory and fell down in a fit, from which he had still not recovered at the end of the war. Ironically Bomber Command probably saved his life; his poor state of health prevented his trial and a possible death sentence at the Nuremberg trials of 1945-6. Twenty-three aircraft failed to return from this mission and 67 were damaged, 43 of them by flak.

The second attack, on 30/31 July, was against Remscheid; 273 bombers took part, led by nine Oboe Mosquitoes. Of the 228 crews claiming to have attacked the objective, photographic reconnaissance suggested that at least 191 had placed their loads within three miles of the aiming point. The centre of Remscheid was completely wiped out and substantial damage was caused to other areas of the town. Once again uncontrollable firestorms accounted for much of the devastation; conflagrations were still sweeping through the shattered streets two days later. Fifteen bombers failed to return from this operation and 12 more were damaged. Eight of the missing aircraft were Stirlings, which were part of a force of 87 sent out by No. 3 Group. Because of their lower speed they had tended to fall behind the time schedule and had been picked off one by one, having been outside the protective screen of Window dropped by the main bomber stream.

Although the effectiveness of Bomber Command's area attacks was growing constantly throughout the spring and summer of 1943, not all the successes were confined to this type of operation. During this period Bomber Command also carried out a series of remarkably successful precision attacks, the most famous of which was the raid against the Ruhr dams on 17 May 1943. The more dramatic story behind the raid is well known, thanks to Paul Brickhill's book *The Dam Busters* and the subsequent film of the same name, but the full amazing story of technical achievement and ingenuity that lay behind it was not revealed until twenty years after the event.

The mission against the Ruhr dams, code-named Operation Upkeep, was the end product of three years' work by Dr Barnes Wallis of Vickers Armstrong, during which he had striven to develop an air-dropped weapon capable of smashing a slab of concrete 130 feet high and varying in thickness from 112 feet at the base to 25 feet at the top. After making extensive tests Wallis calculated that, even if the powerful new RDX explosive were used, such a weapon would have to weigh 70,000 pounds-and even then it would have to be placed with extreme accuracy close to the face of the dam. The only alternative was to devise a weapon which would actually be in contact with the dam at the moment of explosion, in which case a smaller charge would probably be sufficient to produce the necessary shock-waves to effect a breach.

After further tests with models Wallis worked out that the job might be done with as little as 6,000 lb of explosive. To prove the theory he obtained permission to conduct a large-scale experiment against an old dam at Nant-y-gro, across the mouth of a reach of the Rhayader Lake in Radnorshire, Wales. An explosive charge, reduced to scale, was detonated against the 150-foot long structure, which was successfully breached.

While these experiments continued Wallis fought to obtain official backing for his work. Although the various government departments responsible for the conduct of the war were intrigued by the prospect of destroying the Ruhr dams, they were sceptical about the prospect of this being achieved by a bomb — and particularly one which, as Wallis explained, would have to be skipped across the surface of the water like a flat stone in order to get it up against the structure. Nevertheless the experiments carried out so far convinced the authorities at least partially that Wallis had a sound idea, and work was ordered to go ahead on six prototype bombs. These were to be half the size of the projected operational version and were to be dropped from a Wellington, which had its bomb-doors removed to accommodate the weapons. The latter were suspended by their axis on two caliper arms with a belt drive powered by an auxiliary engine in the fuselage. This arrangement was designed to give the bombs a backward spin, which was necessary to make them skip across the lake.

The first test drop was made on 4 December 1942 from a Wellington flown by J. 'Mutt' Summers, Vickers' chief test pilot, with Wallis himself acting as bomb aimer. Four more drops — all of them successful — were made between 12 and 15 December, and after further discussion approval was finally obtained on 26 February 1943 for the execution of Operation Upkeep. A Lancaster squadron was to be specially formed for the purpose and the date selected for the attack was some time in May, when the lakes behind the dams would be full. Less than three months therefore remained in which to design and test the full-scale bombs, train the crews and modify the Lancasters.

The bomb itself was designed and manufactured by Vickers. In its operational form it was a cylinder 6,0 inches long by 50 inches in diameter; its total weight was 9,250 lb, of which 6,600 lb was RDX. The weapon was carried across the bomb-bay of the Lancaster slung between two V-shaped arms, each of which was hinged in a fore and aft direction. At each end of the bomb's casing there was a hollow circular track with a diameter of 20 inches, into which fitted disc wheels carried at the ends of the release mechanism's caliper arms. A VSG hydraulic motor in the fuselage was used to belt-drive one of the discs, imparting the necessary spin to the weapon before release. The idea was to start up the motor about ten minutes before the target was reached, accelerating the spin of the bomb to 500 rpm. When the release toggle was pressed the caliper arms sprang outwards sharply, allowing the weapon to fall freely until it hit the water, still spinning. On contact, the bomb bounced across the surface until it struck the top of the dam; it then bounced back and sank, but its spin propelled it forward under the water until it came into contact with the face of the structure. Three hydrostatic pistols were set to detonate the explosive charge at a depth of thirty feet.

The necessary modifications to the Lancaster were designed by Vickers, but the work was undertaken by Avro. Twenty-three Lancaster Mk IIIs were converted; the first arrived at Farn-borough on 8 April 1943 and the second was delivered to the A&AEE at Boscombe Down for handling trials later that month. As well as the bomb-bay, other modifications included the elimination of the mid-upper gun turret and the inclusion of a large transparent moulding beneath the nose turret. Two spotlights were fitted fore and aft under the fuselage; these were focused to coincide when the aircraft was sixty feet above the water, the exact height from which the bomb had to be dropped. The weapon also had to be released at a speed not exceeding 250 mph and at a distance of between 400 and 450 yards from the dam. To meet the latter requirement a simple triangulation sight was devised. Resembling a coat-hanger, it was lined up by the bomb aimer with the towers at either end of the dams.

The first drop of a prototype bomb was made from a Lancaster on 16 April 1943 off the Kent coast near Reculver. This weapon comprised the cylinder enclosed by a wooden fairing to give it a spherical shape, a design much favoured by Wallis, but on this first test the bomb disintegrated. During a second drop later that day the wooden fairing broke, but the cylinder worked satisfactorily. A third drop was made on 22 April, and once again the weapon disintegrated. After that it was decided to dispense with the wooden fairing, which was simply breaking up on contact with the water. Another test drop was made on 29 April, only three weeks before the date of the attack, and this time everything worked perfectly.

Meanwhile the first of the modified Lancasters had been delivered to No. 617 Squadron at Scampton, which had formed on 21 March 1943 under the leadership of Wing Commander G. P. Gibson. Even Gibson did not know until several weeks later that the unit's task was to breach the Mohne, Eder and Sorpe dams, which together stored more than 300 million tons of water vital to the industries in the Ruhr. Twenty-one aircraft were delivered to the squadron, of which nineteen were earmarked to take part in the attack.

The first Lancaster took off from Scampton at 21.25 on 16 May. Of the nineteen aircraft that set out, two failed to reach the target and returned to base; one of them, flown by Pilot Officer Geoffrey Rice, flew so low as it crossed the Zuyder Zee on its way to Germany that its bomb struck the water and was torn away. Gibson's Lancaster was the first to attack the Mohne Dam, releasing its weapon at 00.28. Four more Lancasters attacked in turn during the next thirty minutes. After the fifth attack the dam burst and Gibson radioed the code-word Nigger back to Scampton, indicating that a breach had been achieved. The remaining aircraft of Gibson's formation carried on to the Eder Dam. The first two bombs failed to breach it, but after the third attack the radio operators at Scampton received the code-word Dinghy, indicating that this part of the mission had also succeeded. Other Lancasters of 617 attacked the Sorpe and Schwelme dams, but failed to destroy them.

Eight Lancasters failed to return from the raid. Five crashed or were shot down on their way to the target; two were shot down during the actual attack, and another was destroyed on the way home. Thirty-two members of the squadron were decorated for their part in the attack, and Gibson himself received the Victoria Cross. After delivering his own attack on the Mohne Dam, Gibson had circled overhead for thirty minutes, drawing the full weight of the enemy anti-aircraft fire on to his own aircraft.

The operation had been a partial success, and a costly one; the night's work had cost No. 617 Squadron almost half its highly trained crews. Nevertheless the decision was taken to retain the squadron as a precision-bombing unit, and on 15/16 July 1943 it returned to operations with a raid on two power stations in northern Italy. All the aircraft landed safely at Blida in North Africa, and during the return flight to the UK on 24/25 July they attacked Leghorn. In August the Squadron moved to Coningsby, and on 15/16 September it used 12,000-lb high capacity bombs (Tallboys) for the first time in an attack on the Dortmund-Ems Canal. This too proved a costly venture. The plan called for the eight Lancasters involved to go in at very low level, dropping their delayed-action bombs from 150 feet. While the attack was in progress the bomber leader — Squadron Leader G. W. Holden, who had taken over command of the squadron from Gibson-was to give directions over the radio, just as his predecessor had done during the dams raid. Before the target was reached, however, Holden's aircraft was hit by flak and blew up, followed in quick succession by four more Lancasters. The three survivors continued, but one was unable to locate the target in appalling visibility and aborted. The other two, flown by Flight Lieutenants Martin and Shannon, managed to bomb the objective in the face of terrific flak; one bomb fell in the canal and the other exploded on the embankment, which did not burst. Once again the squadron had been virtually decimated. The fact that heavy bombers could not operate against heavily defended targets at low level was gradually being hammered home.

The second outstanding precision attack of 1943 took place on the night of 17/18 August. The target was Peenemünde on the shores of the Baltic, the German rocket research establishment. A total of 597 heavy bombers were earmarked for the attack, which was code-named Operation Hydra. The mission involved the precision bombing of a series of selected buildings grouped around three principal aiming points — a difficult task, as the buildings were widely dispersed along a narrow coastal strip and it would be all too easy to waste a great many bombs in the open spaces between them.

The operation was directed by Group Captain J. H. Searby of No. 83 Squadron, Pathfinder Force, who remained over the target throughout the attack, passing instructions over the R/T to the main bomber force. It was the first time that the 'Master Bomber' technique was applied to a major attack. During the raid a new type of marker bomb was used; this was a 250- pounder crammed with impregnated cotton wool, which ignited at 3,000 feet and burned with a brilliant crimson flame for about ten minutes. It was easily recognizable, and the Germans found it extremely difficult to devise an effective decoy.

The attack was highly successful, and Peenemünde suffered heavily. As well as destroying numerous vital sites and installations, the bombs killed a number of top German scientists, setting back the German long-range rocket research programme by as much as six months. Nevertheless the cost to Bomber Command was heavy: 40 aircraft failed to return and 32 others sustained varying degrees of damage.

As the summer of 1943 wore on into autumn, Bomber Command's night offensive crept inexorably eastwards towards the German capital. In September and early October Mannheim and Kassel were heavily bombed in turn and Berlin itself was hit three times, but these early assaults on the capital were only moderately successful. Munich and Dusseldorf were also attacked, and it was during a raid on the latter city that a pilot of No. 61 Squadron, Flight Lieutenant William Reid, won a Victoria Cross. The citation ran as follows:

On the night of November 3rd, 1943, Flight Lieutenant Reid was pilot and Captain of a Lancaster aircraft detailed to attack Dusseldorf.

Shortly after crossing the Dutch coast, the pilot's windscreen was shattered by fire from a Messerschmitt no. Owing to a failure in the heating circuit, the rear gunner's hands were too cold for him to open fire immediately or to operate his microphone and so give warning of danger; but after a brief delay he managed to return the Messerschmitt's fire and it was driven off.

During the fight with the Messerschmitt Flight Lieutenant Reid was wounded in the head, shoulders and hands. The elevator trimming tabs of the aircraft were damaged and it became difficult to control. The rear turret, too, was badly damaged and the communications system and compasses were put out of action. Fight Lieutenant Reid ascertained that his crew were unscathed, and saying nothing about his own injuries, he continued his mission.

Soon afterwards, the Lancaster was attacked by a Focke-Wulf 190. This time, the enemy's fire raked the bomber from stem to stem. The rear gunner replied with his only serviceable gun, but the state of his turret made accurate aiming impossible. The navigator was killed and the wireless operator fatally injured. The mid-upper turret was hit and the oxygen system put out of action. Flight Lieutenant Reid was again wounded and the flight engineer, although hit in the forearm, supplied him with oxygen from a portable supply.

Flight Lieutenant Reid refused to be turned from his objective and Dusseldorf was reached some 50 minutes later. He had memorized his course to the target and had continued in such a normal manner that the bomb-aimer, who was cut off by the failure of the communications system, knew nothing of his captain's injuries or of the casualties to his comrades.

Photographs show that, when the bombs were released, the aircraft was right over the centre of the target.

Steering by the pole star and the moon, Flight Lieutenant Reid then set course for home. He was growing weak from loss of blood. The emergency oxygen supply had given out. With the windscreen shattered, the cold was intense. He lapsed into semi-consciousness. The flight engineer, with some help from the bomb-aimer, kept the Lancaster in the air despite heavy antiaircraft fire over the Dutch coast.

The North Sea crossing was accomplished. An airfield was sighted. The captain revived, resumed control and made ready to land. Ground mist partially obscured the runway lights. The captain was also much bothered by blood from his head wound getting into his eyes, but he made a safe landing although one leg of the damaged undercarriage collapsed when the load came on.

Wounded in two attacks, without oxygen, suffering severely from cold, his navigator dead, his wireless operator fatally wounded, his aircraft crippled and defenceless, Flight Lieutenant Reid showed superb courage and leadership in penetrating a further 200 miles into enemy territory to attack one of the most strongly defended targets in Germany, every additional mile increasing the hazards of the long and perilous journey home. His tenacity and devotion to duty were beyond praise.

*

By the beginning of November 1943 Sir Arthur Harris was firmly convinced that the really decisive phase of the strategic air offensive was about to begin. 'We can wreck Berlin from end to end,' he told Winston Churchill on 3 November, 'if the USAAF will come in on it. It will cost between us 400-500 aircraft. It will cost Germany the war.' Two weeks later, on the night of 18/19 November, Bomber Command struck the opening blow in the Battle of Berlin; the offensive was to last until 24 March 1944, during which period sixteen major operations were mounted against the city. The assault involved the despatch of 9,111 sorties, of which 7,256 were by Lancasters, 1,643 by Halifaxes, 162 by Mosquitoes and 50 by Stirlings. The cost to the RAF was 92 aircraft lost over enemy territory and 954 damaged, of which 95 were destroyed.

The offensive against Berlin, as it turned out, was almost entirely a British effort. The US 8th AAF did not enter the battle until its closing stages, being neither equipped to mount massive night operations nor to undertake — at this stage — deep penetration missions in daylight into enemy territory. It was not until the spring of 1944, when long-range fighter escort became available, that the Americans were in a position to carry out such operations without suffering crippling losses; and not even the mighty war machine of the United States could support indefinitely losses of the magnitude inflicted on the 8th AAF during 1943.

3 - The German Air Defences, 1943-4

At the end of 1942, despite repeated warnings of impending catastrophe from men such as Hans Jeschonnek, Göring's Chief of Staff, German fighter production had still not been given top priority. The danger had been foreseen even earlier by Ernst Udet, former head of the *Luftwaffe's* Technical Office, who in 1941-shortly before his suicide — had urged the industry to 'produce fighters, fighters, fighters!' But his cry had gone unheeded, and in the autumn of 1941 the *Luftwaffe's* production programme envisaged the building of only 360 fighters per month — far too few to meet the demands of the various fronts on which the Germans were committed. Udet's successor, General Erhard Milch, managed to double the fighter output during 1942, and by the end of the year the monthly total was increasing steadily: in February 1943 it stood at 700, in March and April 800, in May 950 and in June 1,000.

It was still not enough. As fast as the fighters were being produced they were being swallowed up by the front-line squadrons in Russia, France and the Low Countries; the defence of the Reich still took second place.

It was only after the massive Anglo-American attacks on Hamburg — accompanied by the extensive use of Window, which rendered the German fighter control system almost impotent during this period — that the *Luftwaffe* chiefs joined forces in an attempt to convince Hitler and Göring that the German day-and night-fighter forces must be greatly strengthened as a matter of urgency. Göring at last began to appreciate their point of view. Hitler, on the other hand, remained inflexible.

Terror [he stated] can only be broken by terror! Everything else is nonsense. The British will only be halted when their own cities are destroyed. I can only win the war by dealing out more destruction to the enemy than he does to us ... In all epochs that has been the case, and it is just the same in the air. Otherwise our people will turn mad, and in the course of time lose all confidence in the Luftwaffe ...

Despite Hitler's firm commitment to the idea of reprisals, however, the inevitable decision to strengthen the German air defences was not long in coming. On 28 July 1943, in the wake of the second heavy RAF attack on Hamburg, Göring issued instructions through Milch that the German aircraft industry should concentrate on fighter production with immediate effect. At the same time work was accelerated on new types of airborne interception radar which would not be subject to Window jamming.

Bomber Command's massive onslaught on Germany's major cities had disastrous consequences for General Josef Kammhuber, Commander of Fliegerkorps XII *and the Luftwaffe's* night-fighter force. Since his appointment in 1940 Kammhuber had striven to weld the German night defences into as efficient an organization as his resources would permit. He was the architect of the 'Himmelbett' system, a network of overlapping air-defence zones stretching from north to south across the length of occupied Europe, and was a firm advocate of night intruder operations as a means of inflicting the maximum possible damage on Bomber Command over its own territory — although what might have become the most potent weapon in his arsenal was knocked from his hand when Hitler personally called a halt to intruder missions over England. Despite the obstacles that confronted him one after the other, Kammhuber had persevered with his task until by the spring of 1943 he had five *Geschwader* (Wings) and 400 twin-engined night-fighters under his command on bases ranging from Holland to the Mediterranean.

Kammhuber, however, was the first to realize that 400 night-fighters were not enough to counter the massive armadas of four-engined bombers which were beginning to make deeper inroads into German territory night after night. He consequently proposed a major extension of the Himmelbett air-defence system, with eighteen night-fighter *Geschwader* covering the whole of Germany. The aircraft would be fitted with improved AI (radar) equipment and the ground radar network would also be modernized, even though this would mean a major upheaval in the German electronics industry.

Kammhuber's proposals appeared to provide the only logical solution to the problem of defending Germany at night, and they were partially supported by Göring. All it needed now was for Hitler to set his seal on the plan — and it was here that the first blow fell. Kammhuber had begun his report with some facts and figures on Allied aircraft production, stressing that the Americans were producing 5,000 combat aircraft per month and that a large proportion of these were earmarked for service in the European theatre. Hitler however dismissed the figures as ridiculous. If they were correct, he raged, he would have to withdraw every last fighter from the various fronts and assign them to home defence. But no one could convince him that the figures were correct, or that the Luftwaffe's night-fighters were not already destroying enough enemy bombers to cripple the Allied air offensive. The proposals were swept aside and now Göring also turned on Kammhuber, reproaching the general for making 'senseless demands' — which, until the stormy interview with the Führer, the Reichsmarschall had been quite prepared to meet.

After that Kammhuber's decline from power was rapid, especially when Bomber Command's use of Window in July 1943 rendered the Himmelbett system of close fighter control virtually impotent. A few weeks later he was replaced as GOC *Fliegerkorps* XII by Major-General Josef Schmid, and in November he was also relieved of his appointment as commander of the night-fighter force.

Another direct result of the great assault on Hamburg was a proposal, made initially by a Colonel von Lossberg of the General Staff, that the night-fighters be released from the confines of the Himmelbett zones, where their movements were too restricted, and instead mix freely with the bomber stream. This idea was approved by a committee composed of Milch, Colonel-General Weise, Generals Kammhuber and Galland, and Major Werner Streib, the commander of *Nachtjagdgeschwader* i. Finally it was decided to increase the strength of *Jagdgeschwader* 300, formed a month earlier under the command of Major Hajo Herrmann. This was the pioneer *Wilde Sau* (Wild Boar) unit; equipped with single-engined fighter aircraft, its task was to patrol directly over the German cities, the pilots endeavouring to pick out enemy bombers in the glare of searchlights and fires.

The first major *Wilde Sau* operation carried out by the newly strengthened JG 300 brought disappointing results. It took place on the night of 17/18 August 1943, when Bomber Command attacked the rocket research centre at Peenemünde. Thanks to a handful of Mosquitoes, which dropped masses of flares over Berlin, the German fighter controllers were led to believe that the capital was the target, and 148 fighters of JG 300 patrolled overhead for the best part of an hour without sighting a single enemy aircraft. The ruse was recognized for what it was only after the first bombs had gone down on Peenemünde, and by the time the fighters arrived on the scene most of the heavy bombers were already making for home.

The next operation, during the RAF attack on Berlin on the night of 23/24 August, was more successful. This time the German controllers knew at least an hour in advance that Berlin was the target, and when the bombers arrived over the capital the night-fighter *Gruppen* were waiting for them. Thanks mainly to the *Wilde Sau* tactics, the first three major raids on Berlin — on 23 August and 1 and 4 September — cost Bomber Command 123 aircraft destroyed, together with a further 114 damaged. Far from delivering the shattering blow to German morale which Air Marshal Harris had envisaged, this opening phase of the Battle of Berlin was regarded by the Germans as a victory for the defences. In September Hajo Herrmann was promoted to the rank of Lieutenant-Colonel, and the strength of the *Wilde Sau* force was further increased to three *Geschwader*, but although the increase looked impressive enough on paper each *Geschwader* had in fact only enough aircraft to equip a single *Gruppe*. The others had to make use of aircraft belonging to day-fighter units, many of which soon began to suffer badly from overwork.

Most of the *Wilde Sau* successes were achieved on clear autumn nights, when the fighter pilots — cruising high above the level of searchlights and flak — had little difficulty in picking out bombers silhouetted against the glow beneath. With the onset of bad weather during the winter months their task became infinitely harder, and attrition took a severe toll of the single-engined fighters, most of which were not equipped for blind flying. Landing accidents were frequent, and on more than one occasion 25 out of 60 aircraft sent out on operations were destroyed in a single night. In March 1944 the *Wilde Sau* force-which had now reached the status of an Air Division — was finally disbanded and its pilots retained for day-fighter duties.

Meanwhile development of advanced radio and radar equipment had continued to receive high priority during the winter of 1943-4. In October 1943 the night-fighter units began to receive the first of the new FUG 220 Lichtenstein SN-2 airborne interception radars, developed by Telefunken and free from both electronic and Window jamming. It had a maximum range of four miles and a minimum range of 450 yards, and it was not long before some night-fighter crews began to register a formidable number of successes with its help. In the autumn of 1943 two more homing devices were also developed for use by night-fighters, the FUG 350 Naxos z and the FUG 227 Flensburg. The former enabled the fighters to home on transmissions from the RAF'S H2S blindbombing radar, and the latter was designed to lock on to radiations from the Monica tail warning radar carried by the heavy bombers.

In the early months of 1944 the Allies knew very little about this new equipment, and went to great lengths to gather reliable intelligence data on it. The first real clue came by chance, during an examination of film taken by an American fighter during a strafing run over a German airfield. The somewhat blurred photographs revealed a Junkers 88 night-fighter sporting a bulky array of aerials on its nose, and analysis by electronics experts showed that these were suitable for an AI radar operating in the 100 megacycles band. Work on countermeasures equipment began at once, but was beset by various difficulties. Then came a real windfall. On 13 July 1944 a Junkers 88G night-fighter on patrol over the North Sea made a serious navigational error and landed at Woodbridge in Suffolk. The aircraft was equipped with both SN-2 radar and the Flensburg homing device, which were quickly put through the mill by the scientists of the Telecommunications Research Establishment. As a result of their findings a new type of Window was devised. Cut to a longer wavelength than the earlier model, it was first used on 23 July 1944 during a night raid on Kiel. However it was soon found that although the new Window rendered the SN-2 radar useless inside the bomber stream, it was still ineffective against aircraft above, ahead of or upwind of the stream. The scientists' answer to this deficiency was Piperack, which was fitted to the special countermeasures aircraft of No. 100 Group and was designed to produce clutter on the enemy AI radar screens.

Early in 1944 the Germans began work on two new types of AI radar, the FUG 218 Neptun VR and the FUG 228 Lichtenstein SN-3. The former worked in the 163-187 megacycles band, the latter in the 100-112 megacycles band, and the frequencies of both could be altered in the air to make jamming more difficult. Production of the SN-3 had already started when the Allies found an effective means of jamming the German Freya ground radar, which worked on the same waveband, so further work on the SN-3AI set was stopped and production concentrated on Neptun. This was first used operationally in February 1945, but the

Allies quickly discovered that it was vulnerable to Window of the right length and within three weeks effective countermeasures had been devised against it.

Throughout the great battles in the night sky over Germany during 1943-4, two principal aircraft types formed the backbone of the *Luftwaffe*'s night-fighter force. These were the Junkers Ju 88 and its variants and the Messerschmitt Bf 110. During 1944 alone 2,518 Ju 88s and 1,525 Bf 110s were built for the night-fighter role. Production of the Bf 110 would have reached the 2,000 mark but for Allied bombing during February 1944, when 465 machines of this type were destroyed in the factories.

In the first half of 1943 General Kammhuber had pressed strongly for the production of new twin-engined types designed specifically for night-fighting. At the forefront of these was the Heinkel He 219 Uhu (Owl), the prototype of which had flown in November 1942 after months of delay caused by lack of interest in the German Air Ministry. By April 1943 300 examples had been ordered; Kammhuber wanted 2,000, but in the event only 294 were built before the end of the war. Formidably armed with six 20-mm cannon and equipped with the latest AI radar, the He 219 would undoubtedly have torn great gaps in Bomber Command's ranks had it been available in quantity. Among other innovations the Uhu was fitted with ejection seats fired by compressed air. The first ever ejection under combat conditions was made from one of these machines in 1944.

Another promising night-fighter that fell by the wayside was the Focke-Wulf Ta 154 Moskito. Like its British namesake the Ta 154 was of all-wood construction. It was ordered into production in November 1943, but in June the following year two early production Ta 154A-IS were accidentally destroyed — one when it fell apart because faulty glue had been used in its assembly, the other when its flaps broke away during an approach to land — and as a result the production order was cancelled.

Since specialized night-fighters were practically non-existent, the *Luftwaffe's* night-fighter arm was forced to rely almost entirely on modifications to existing types. One such was the Dornier Do 217, the E-2 version of which was selected for conversion to the night-fighter role in 1942. Basically the conversion involved replacing the glazed nose of the

Do 217 bomber with a more streamlined 'solid' fairing containing additional guns. One hundred and fifty-seven 1-2s were converted and re-designated Do 217J-1 or J-2; the former was employed on intruder work over the UK while the j-2 had its bomb-bay faired over and was equipped with Lichtenstein AI radar. Armament was four 20-mm cannon and four 7.9-mm machine-guns in the nose, and there was provision for a 13-mm gun in a ventral position.

By the end of 1943, the offensive armament of most German night-fighters had been supplemented by an ingenious gun mounting known as *Schräge Musik* (literally: slanting music). Devised by a sergeant armourer named Paul Mahle, it involved the mounting of two 20-mm cannon, their muzzles pointing upwards at a fixed angle, on a wooden platform in the upper fuselage of a night-fighter. This arrangement enabled the fighter to take advantage of a bomber's blind spot and attack it from directly below with the aid of a reflector sight mounted in the cockpit roof.

Schräge Musik was used for the first time on the night of 17/18 August during the raid on Peenemünde, when two crews of II/NJG 5 destroyed six RAF bombers in the space of thirty minutes. The German airmen reported that the Halifaxes and Lancasters were extremely vulnerable to this form of attack. The large area of their wings was impossible to miss, and since the wings contained the fuel tanks a relatively short burst was usually enough to set a bomber on fire. Between the night of the Peenemünde raid and 2 October, the crews of II/NJG 5 scored eighteen victories with the aid of *Schräge Musik* for no loss to themselves.

Despite the problems of equipment and organization that handicapped the German night-fighter force, its success rate reached an unprecedented peak in the spring of 1944. In the course of three big air battles over darkened Germany, Bomber Command suffered crippling losses. On the night of February 19/20, 78 out of a force of 823 heavy bombers despatched to attack Leipzig failed to return; 72 more were destroyed during the final big assault on Berlin on 24/25 March; and then, five nights later, came the most catastrophic raid of all.

At nightfall on 30 March, 795 heavy bombers set out from their English bases to attack the vital industrial centre and railway junction of Nuremberg. The night was cloudless and calm, and across a great arc of Europe stretching across Holland, Belgium, northern France and north-west Germany the *Luftwaffe* night-fighter crews were at cockpit readiness. At 22.00 reports began to come in of small-scale attacks by Mosquitoes on several airfields in Holland and of minelaying operations over the North Sea, but the GOC I Fighter Corps, Major-General Josef Schmid, realized that these were simply diversions and kept his night-fighters on the ground. Then, at 22.30, the German coastal radar stations detected a major raid building up on the other side of the Channel, and a few minutes later the bomber stream was reported to be heading south-eastwards towards Belgium. At 23.00 Schmid finally ordered his fighters into the air.

This time, instead of carrying out the normal procedure and making several abrupt changes of course to confuse the defences, the bomber stream steered due east for 150 miles after making landfall on the enemy coast, and the night-fighters had no difficulty in locating their targets. The route to Nuremberg was marked by a series of fiery beacons as one heavy bomber after another fell burning from the sky. From all over Germany the night-fighter *Gruppen* converged on the bomber stream. One crew of I/NJG 6 destroyed no fewer than seven bombers in two sorties; two more crews of II/NJG 5 accounted for four each, and a third crew of the same unit destroyed three, all as a result of attacks from below with the aid of *Schräge Musik*.

The attacks intensified as the bomber stream approached the target area. One Halifax of No. 578 Squadron, flown by Pilot Officer C. J. Barton, was attacked by a Junkers 88 some 70 miles from Nuremberg, and the night-fighter's first burst of fire shattered the intercom system. A Messerschmitt 210 then joined in the battle, putting the Halifax's machine-guns out of action. The attacks continued almost without pause as the bomber struggled on, and in the confusion at the height of the battle the navigator, bombardier and wireless operator, misinterpreting a hand signal from the pilot and believing the aircraft was about to crash, took to their parachutes.

Barton was now faced with an impossible situation. His aircraft was badly damaged, his navigator was gone and he was unable to communicate with the rest of the crew. If he continued the mission his defenceless aircraft would be completely at the mercy of hostile fighters when silhouetted against the fires of the target area, and if he survived he would have to make a four-and-a-half-hour journey home on three engines across heavily defended territory. Despite everything Barton decided to press on. The aircraft reached Nuremberg without further incident, and the pilot released the bomb load himself.

As Barton turned for home the propeller of the damaged engine, which was vibrating badly, flew off. To make matters worse, it was found that two of the fuel tanks had suffered battle damage and were leaking. He nevertheless stuck to his course and, in spite of strong headwinds, successfully avoided the most dangerous defensive areas along his route. He eventually crossed the English coast only ninety miles north of his base at Burn, in Yorkshire.

By this time the fuel supply was almost exhausted, and before a suitable landing place could be found the remaining port engine stopped. With two dead engines on the same wing the damaged aircraft was almost uncontrollable, and it was too low to be abandoned successfully. As Barton ordered the three remaining crew members to take up crash stations the starboard outer engine also stopped. With only one engine working the pilot made a desperate attempt to avoid some houses. The Halifax crashed on open ground and broke up. Barton was killed, but the three members of his crew survived to tell the full story of his gallantry. He was awarded a posthumous Victoria Cross.

Barton's Halifax was one of twelve that crashed on return to England. For Bomber Command the cost of the Nuremberg raid was stupendous: 95 bombers failed to return and 71 were damaged. The loss — 11.8 per cent of the attacking force — was the highest ever sustained by the Command. It was the greatest victory achieved by the German night-fighters during the war; it was also their last.

4 - The Daylight Offensive, 1943-4

17 August 1943, 08.00 Hours.

To the fighter controllers of the Luftwaffe's 1st Air Division it was apparent that something big was in the wind. For some time the German monitoring stations along the Channel coast had been reporting unusual activity on the airfields of the US 8th Air Force in East Anglia, and there were further intelligence indications that the Americans were about to carry out a deep-penetration mission into German territory.

At 09.00 the German radar stations reported a large raid building up over the English coast. Meanwhile several *Luftwaffe* fighter *Gruppen* were being hurriedly moved from their bases on the North Sea coast to new locations west of Rheims. The fighters had scarcely been refuelled and rearmed when, at 10.00, 146 B-17s and B-24S crossed the Dutch coast and headed inland, escorted by a massive formation of Spitfires and p-47 Thunderbolts. The whole armada was shadowed by several Focke-Wulf 190s of II/JG 1, which remained at a respectful distance and made no move to attack.

A few minutes later the Allied formation turned south and crossed Belgium at 20,000 feet. Then, within sight of the German frontier, came the moment the *Luftwaffe* had been waiting for: the Spitfires and Thunderbolts, at the limit of their combat radius turned back. The Focke-Wulfs immediately climbed hard until they were ahead of and above the bomber formation, then peeled off to make a frontal attack. Sweeping under the bombers like a whirlwind, they climbed up to make a second attack. Four B-17S dropped out of formation, burning fiercely; they were followed within minutes by three more. As one fighter *Gruppe* exhausted its ammunition it was replaced by another. The sky was filled with twisting Messerschmitts and Focke-Wulfs and smoke trails.

For ninety minutes the battle continued without respite as the heavy bombers battled their way through to the target: the Messerschmitt aircraft factory at Regensburg-Prüfening. In their wake, like grim markers, lay the shattered wrecks of fourteen of their number. After carrying out their attack the bombers turned south, heading for the

Mediterranean and North Africa. On the way out of the target area ten more B-17S fell to the guns of the fighters of *Luftflotte* 2, representing a total loss of twenty-four aircraft — not to mention many more severely damaged.

The carnage of the Regensburg mission was graphically described by the co-pilot of a Fortress in one of the rear Groups, one that suffered particularly heavily.

At 1017 hours, near Woensdrecht, I saw the first flak blossom out in our vicinity, light and inaccurate. A few minutes later, two FW 190s appeared at one o'clock level and whizzed through the formation ahead of us in a frontal attack, nicking two B-17S in the wings and breaking away beneath us in half rolls. Smoke immediately trailed from both B-17S, but they held their stations. As the fighters passed us at a high rate of closure, the guns of our Groups went into action. The pungent smell of burnt powder filled our cockpit, and the B-17 trembled to the recoil of nose and ball turret guns. I saw pieces fly off the wing of one of the fighters before they passed from view.

Here was early action. The members of the crew sensed trouble. There was something desperate about the way those two fighters came in fast right out of their climb without any preliminaries ... Three minutes later the gunners reported fighters climbing up from all around the clock, singly and in pairs, both FW 109s and Me 109s. Every gun from every B-17 in our Group was firing, crisscrossing our patch of sky with tracers. Both sides got hurt in this clash, with two Fortresses from our low squadron and one from the Group ahead falling out of formation on fire with crews bailing out, and several fighters heading for the deck in flames with their pilots lingering behind under dirty yellow parachutes. I noticed an Me 110 sitting out of range on our right. He was to stay with us all the way to the target, apparently reporting our position to fresh squadrons waiting for us down the road. At the sight of all these fighters I had the distinct feeling of being trapped. The life expectancy of our Group suddenly seemed very short, since it appeared that the fighters were passing up the preceding Groups in order to take a cut at us.

Swinging their yellow noses round in a wide U-turn, a twelve-ship squadron of Me 109s came in from twelve o'clock in pairs and in fours, and the main event was on. A shining silver object sailed over our right wing. I recognized it as a main exit door. Seconds later, a dark object came hurtling through the formation, barely missing several props. It was a man, clasping his knees to his head, revolving like a diver in a triple somersault. I didn't see his chute open.

A B-17 turned gradually out of the formation to the right, maintaining altitude. In a split second, the B-17 completely disappeared in a brilliant explosion, from which the only remains were four small balls of fire, the fuel tanks, which were quickly consumed as they fell earthwards. Our airplane was endangered by falling debris. Emergency hatches, exit doors, prematurely opened parachutes, bodies, and assorted fragments of B-17S and Hun fighters breezed past us in the slipstream.

I watched two fighters explode not far beneath, disappearing in sheets of orange flame, B-17S dropping out in every state of distress, from engines on fire to control surfaces shot away, friendly and enemy parachutes floating down, and, on the green carpet far behind us, numerous funeral pyres of smoke from fallen fighters, marking our trail. The sight was fantastic: it surpassed fiction.

On we flew through the strewn wake of a desperate air battle, where disintegrating aircraft were commonplace and sixty chutes in the air at one time were hardly worth a second look. I watched a B-17 turn slowly out to the right with its cockpit a mass of flames. The co-pilot crawled out of his window, held on with one hand, reached back for his chute, buckled it on, let go, and was whisked back into the horizontal stabilizer. I believe the impact killed him. His chute didn't open.

Ten minutes, twenty minutes, thirty minutes, and still no letup in the attacks. The fighters queued up like a bread line and let us have it. Each second of time had a cannon shell in it. Our B-17 shook steadily with the fire of its .50s, and the air inside was heavy with smoke. It was cold in the cockpit, but when I looked across at the pilot I saw that sweat was pouring off his forehead and over his oxygen mask. He turned the controls over to me for a while. It was a blessed relief to concentrate on holding station in formation instead of watching those everlasting fighters boring in. It was possible to forget the fighters. Then the top turret gunner's muzzles would pound away a foot above my head, giving a realistic imitation of cannon shells exploding in the cockpit, while I gave an even better imitation of a man jumping six inches out of his seat.

A B-17 of the Group ahead, with its right Tokyo tanks on fire, dropped back to about 200 feet above our right wing and stayed there while seven of the crew successively bailed out. Four went out the bomb bay and executed delayed jumps, one bailed from the nose, opened his chute prematurely and nearly fouled the tail. Another went out the left waist gun opening, delaying his chute opening for a safe interval. The tail gunner jumped out of his hatch, apparently pulling the ripcord before he was clear of the ship. His chute opened instantaneously, barely missing the tail, and jerked him so hard that both his shoes came off. He hung limp in the harness, whereas the others had shown immediate signs of life after their chutes opened, shifting around in the harness. The B-17 then dropped back in a medium spiral and I did not see the pilots leave. I saw it just before it passed from view, several thousand feet below us, with its right wing a sheet of yellow flame.

After we had been under constant attack for a solid hour, it appeared certain that our Group was faced with annihilation. Seven of us had been shot down, the sky was still mottled with rising fighters, and it was only 1120 hours, with target-time still thirty-five minutes away. I doubt if a man in the Group visualized the possibility of our getting much further without one hundred per cent loss. I know that I had long since mentally accepted the fact of death, and that it was simply a question of the next second or the next minute. I learned firsthand that a man can resign himself to the certainty of death without becoming panicky. Our Group firepower was reduced thirty-three per cent; ammunition was running low. Our tail guns had to be replenished from another gun station. Gunners were becoming exhausted.

One B-17 dropped out of formation and put its wheels down while the crew bailed out. Three Me 109s circled it closely but held their fire, apparently ensuring that no-one stayed in the ship to try for home. Near the IP, at 1150 hours, one hour and a half after the first of at least 200 individual fighter attacks, the pressure eased off, although hostiles were still in the vicinity. We turned at the IP at 1154 hours with fourteen B-17s left in the Group, two of which were badly crippled. They dropped out soon after bombing the target and headed for Switzerland.

Weather over the target, as on the entire trip, was ideal. Flak was negligible. The Group got its bombs away promptly on the leader. As we turned and headed for the Alps, I got a grim satisfaction out of seeing a rectangular column of smoke rising straight up from the Me 109 shops. The rest of the trip was a marked anticlimax. A few more fighters pecked at us on the way to the Alps. A town in the Brenner Pass tossed up a lone burst of futile flak. We circled over Lake Garda long enough to give the cripples a chance to join the family, and we were on our way towards the Mediterranean in a gradual descent. The prospect of ditching as we approached North Africa, short of fuel, and the sight of other B-17S falling into the drink, seemed trivial matters after the vicious nightmare of the long trip across southern Germany. We felt the reaction of men who had not expected to see another sunset.

At 18.15 hours, with red lights showing on all the fuel tanks in my ship, the seven B-17S of the Group which were still in formation circled over a North African airdrome and landed. Our crew was unscratched. Sole damage to the airplane: a bit of ventilation around the tail from flak and 20-mm shells. We slept on the hard ground under the wings of our B-17, but the good earth felt softer than a silk pillow.

For the 8th Air Force the ordeal of 17 August was not yet over. In the early afternoon 229 Fortresses crossed the Dutch coast *en route* to bomb the ball-bearing factories at Schweinfurt. On this occasion determined fighter attacks began as soon as the formation reached German territory. The *Gruppen* attacked in pairs, one engaging the Allied fighter escort and the other the bombers. At times more than 300 German fighters were in the air, and fierce battles raged along the route to the target. In addition to cannon and machine-guns, some of the fighters were armed with 21 -cm rockets, slung under the wings in two tubes. A direct hit by one of these was enough to tear a bomber apart, and several B-I 7s were lost by this means. The fighter attacks intensified after the Americans' P-47 escort turned for home; 36 Fortresses were shot down, bringing the 8th's total loss for the day to 60 bombers. Over 100 more were damaged, many of them so severely that they had to be written off. After this mauling it was to be five weeks before the American heavy bombers carried out any more long-range missions over Germany.

For the 8th Bomber Command the attacks on Schweinfurt and Regensburg — known as the 'Anniversary Raids' because they took place exactly one year after the start of the American daylight offensive over Occupied Europe — marked the climax of a tragic year. Although 1943 had begun encouragingly enough for the Americans, with the almost unopposed raid on Wilhelmshaven in January, it was not long before the determined packs of *Luftwaffe* fighter pilots shattered the myth that large formations of heavy bombers, without fighter escort and relying entirely on their considerable defensive armament, could operate deep inside enemy territory without suffering serious losses. In the days that followed the Wilhelmshaven mission, however, it was the weather and not the *Luftwaffe* that formed the main obstacle to the 8th's bombing programme, with rain, sleet and freezing layers of cloud extending over the whole area of the North Sea. In seventeen days only one attack was carried out, in conditions of severe icing and temperatures that dropped as low as 45 degrees below zero. This raid took place on 4 February, and the target was the port of Emden. Because of the freezing conditions dense vapour trails formed behind the American formation, enabling the enemy fighters to concentrate on it without difficulty. Fifty fighters, including eight Messerschmitt 110s of a night-fighter unit, engaged the bombers over the north coast of Germany and a fierce air battle developed. Six Fortresses were shot down, but the Germans also suffered heavily, losing eight fighters. Many more were damaged as they manoeuvred around the bomber formation, trying to find a blind spot from which to carry out their attacks.

On 16 February eight more bombers were lost during an attack on the locks leading to the basin of the St Nazaire u-boat base on the French coast. Ten days later another 8th Bomber Command formation battled its way through intense opposition to attack Wilhelmshaven for a second time. Seven bombers were lost. The end of one of them was described by Lieutenant Heinz Knoke, flying a Messerschmitt 109 of II/JG 2.

I come in for a second frontal attack, this time from a little below. I keep on firing until I have to swerve to avoid a collision. My salvoes register this time. I drop away below. As I swing round I turn my head. Flames are spreading along the bottom of the fuselage of my Liberator. It sheers away from the formation in a wide sweep to the right.

Twice more I come in to attack, this time diving from above the tail. I am met by heavy defensive fire. My plane shudders under the recoil from the two cannon and the 13-millimetre guns. I watch my cannon shell-bursts rake along the top of the fuselage and right wing, and I hang on to the stick with both hands. The fire spreads along the right wing. The inside engine stops. Suddenly the wing breaks off altogether. The body of the stricken monster plunges vertically, spinning into the depths. A long black trail of smoke marks its descent. One of the crew attempts to bail out. But his parachute is in flames. Poor devil! The body somersaults and falls to the ground like a stone.

At an altitude of 3,000 feet there is a tremendous explosion, which causes the spinning fuselage to disintegrate. Fragments of blazing wreckage land on a farm 200 or 300 yards from the Zwischenahn airfield, and the exploding fuel tanks sets the farm buildings on fire ...

Despite the losses suffered in these early raids on 'fringe' targets lying round the perimeter of the German homeland, it was decided early in March to carry out the first of 8th Bomber Command's deep-penetration missions against a German objective. On the 4th, four Groups took off from their English bases to attack the big railway marshalling yards at Hamm, a target that had been frequently visited by the RAF. The operation was hampered by bad weather: two of the Groups bombed the shipyards at Rotterdam, another returned to base with its bombs still on board, and only one — consisting of 16 bombers — reached the target. This lone Group achieved an excellent bombing concentration, but four of its aircraft were shot down.

The next four missions were all against rail targets, including the marshalling yards at Rennes, hit by fifty B-17S on 8 March. Then, on the 18th, came the biggest raid so far: 97 heavy bombers — 73 Fortresses and 24 Liberators, the largest force that the 8th Bomber Command had yet sent out to strike at one target — attacked the Vulcan Shipbuilding yards at Vegesack, on the Weser south of Bremen. The next day Wilhelmshaven was once again the target, followed in quick succession by the marshalling yards and repair ships at Rouen and the shipyards at Rotterdam. Eight bombers failed to return from these three missions, the last two of which were strongly escorted by Spitfires and Thunderbolts.

The next objective slated for a major attack by the 8th Air Force was the Renault works, in the suburbs of Paris. This target, wrecked by RAF Bomber Command on the night of 3/4 March 1942, had been completely rebuilt by the Germans in nine months — using French money and labour — and was now turning out 1,500 tanks and trucks per month for the *Wehrmacht*, which represented ten per cent of the enemy's total production in this field.

At 13.50 on 4 April 1943, 85 B-17S crossed Dieppe at 25,000 feet *en route* to Paris, clearly visible as a dark patch nestling in the loops of the Seine 95 miles to the south. At 14.00 the Spitfire squadrons of Fighter

Command accompanying the bombers turned back, but as the Fortresses flew on unescorted there was still no sign of any enemy fighters: the *Luftwaffe* had been lured north by three diversionary attacks, carried out by No. 2 Group RAF Bomber Command. At 14.14 the B-17S were over the target, and in the seven minutes that followed the Groups dropped 251 tons of high explosive on it. Enemy fighters appeared for the first time as the bombers swung northwards towards the coast, and determined attacks persisted until the B-17S made rendezvous with more Spitfire squadrons over Rouen. Four bombers were lost, but reconnaissance showed that the Renault factory had once again been devastated.

The 8th's raids continued to grow in size — and in cost. On 17 April 115 B-17S took off to attack the Focke-Wulf aircraft plant at Bremen. Eight of the bombers aborted, but the remaining 107 battled their way through fierce opposition to the target. Nevertheless 16 Fortresses failed to return from this mission, making it the costliest so far undertaken by the Americans. By this time two factors — both by-products of the weather over western Europe — were beginning to hamper daylight bombing operations to a noticeable extent. First of all, in early spring the days were still not long enough to permit the American crews — who could not fly in formation in the dark and were not trained for night landings — to attack their targets in Germany outside a limited period midway between dawn and dusk. This period usually tended to coincide with maximum cloud development in the target area, so that visual identification of the target was hampered. Secondly, and for the same reason, the Germans were able to calculate the probable time of an American attack quite accurately and assemble their fighters accordingly. The *Gruppen* needed to be on alert only from about three hours after sunrise until three hours before sunset. The overall result was that the Americans met with stronger opposition than ever before during April and May 1943, and their losses rose to a serious level.

Nevertheless by the middle of May the 8th Air Force had sufficient aircraft and crews operational in England to carry out a long-awaited experiment: the mounting of simultaneous large-scale attacks on several different targets. The first such mission took place on 14 May, when over 200 Fortresses and Liberators were despatched in the space of four hours to attack Ijmuiden, Antwerp, Courtrai and Kiel. The diversity of the attacks caused some confusion among the German fighter controllers. Nevertheless the *Luftwaffe* hotly contested the Kiel attack, which was by far the biggest of the four, and eleven aircraft were shot down. The German fighters accounted for five out of seventeen B-24 Liberators which took part. Flying at a lower level than the

Fortresses, they were singled out for concentrated attack. The pilot of one B-24 described the engagement:

Three of them started at us. Our top turret gunner picked out the leader and let him have about fifty rounds from each gun. The copilot saw black smoke pour from the nacelle and the plane go into a spin. Despite the temperature of 20 degrees below zero Centigrade I was sweating like mad. I had on a pair of winter flying boots and nothing else except regular dress, which was wringing wet.

Two more fighters came in from the nose. I could see them firing their cannons, so I pushed forward on the stick with all my might. We went down like a brick-built privy and they whizzed past us, barely missing the top of our wing. One of them took along several of our slugs with him, because our tracers were seen to go through his fuselage. When I pulled out of that dive, our top turret gunner was thrown from his turret, as was the tail gunner. All the other members of the crew were thrown about a bit. But the Jerries had missed us, and that was the important thing.

During May 1943 both RAF Bomber Command and the 8th Air Force carried out an intensive series of attacks on power stations in Holland. All these missions were flown in daylight, and the cost in aircraft and crews was high. On 3 May, for example, eleven Venturas of No. 487 (RNZAF) Squadron, led by Squadron Leader L. H. Trent, took off from their base at Methwold in Norfolk to attack the main power station in Amsterdam. Apart from disrupting the power supply to German-controlled industries in the area, the raid was designed to encourage Dutch workers in their resistance to enemy pressure. The importance of bombing the target, which was heavily defended, was strongly impressed on the crews taking part in the operation, and before take-off Trent told his deputy that he intended to go in whatever happened.

Everything went well until the eleven Venturas and their fighter escort were over the Dutch coast, when one of the bombers was hit by flak and had to turn back. A minute later large numbers of enemy fighters appeared; these engaged the Spitfire escort, which soon lost touch with the Venturas. The latter closed up tightly for mutual protection and started their run towards the target, expecting to rendezvous with more friendly fighters over Amsterdam, but the fighters had arrived in the target area much too soon and had been recalled.

Within moments the Venturas were being savagely attacked by 20 Messerschmitts and Focke-Wulfs. One after the other, six of the bombers went down in flames in the space of four minutes. The remaining four, with Trent at their head, continued doggedly towards the target. The dwindling formation now ran into murderous anti-aircraft fire, which accounted for two more Venturas. Trent and the other surviving crew made accurate bombing runs, harrassed all the time by enemy fighters that braved their own flak to press home their attacks. Trent got in a lucky burst with his nose gun at a FW 190, which flicked into a spin and crashed. A moment later the other Ventura received a direct hit and exploded. Trent turned away from the target area, but his aircraft too was hit and began to break up. Trent and his navigator were thrown clear and became prisoners of war; the other two crew members were killed. After the war, when the full story of the raid emerged, Trent was awarded the Victoria Cross.

Another heavily defended target was the Velsen generating station at Ijmuiden, which was attacked twice early in May by the RAF. On the 14th it was the turn of the Americans, when twelve B-26 Marauders of the 322nd Bombardment Group (Medium) took off from their base at Great Saling to attack this objective. The 322nd, which had arrived in Britain on 8 March, had great faith in its B-26s, which had served extremely well in the low-level attack role in the Pacific. Some officers, however, believed that the German light flak defences — which were far stronger than anything encountered in the Pacific — would make unescorted low-level attack missions over Europe suicidal. Nevertheless low-level training went ahead, and the Group's first combat mission was scheduled for 14 May.

Of the twelve B-26s that took off one aborted and the others unloaded their delayed-action bombs squarely on the target. Although all the aircraft suffered battle damage to some extent, their crews were jubilant: they were convinced that the objective had been destroyed. When reconnaissance photographs were developed the next day, however, the Americans were astonished; no damage at all had been inflicted on the power station. It appeared that the enemy had rushed special bomb disposal squads into the area to disarm the bombs, which had been fitted with thirty-minute fuses.

It was accordingly decided to mount a second operation against Ijmuiden on 17 May, although the commander of the 322nd protested that another mission at low level against the same target was almost certain to end in disaster. The Group's Senior Intelligence Officer, Major Alfred H. von Kelnitz, was of the same opinion. On the morning of the projected attack he wrote a strong memo entitled 'Extreme Danger in Contemplated Mission', in which he pointed out that after the RAF raids of 2 and 5 May, as well as the 322nd's attack of the 14th, the Germans would be ready and waiting. 'For God's sake,' he pleaded, 'get fighter cover!'

But fighter cover was not available, and the 322nd's co, Lieutenant-Colonel Robert M. Stillman, was forced to mount the attack without it. Six aircraft, led by Stillman himself, were to attack Ijmuiden. Six more, led by Lieutenant-Colonel W. R. Purinton, were to attack a power station in Haarlem. The twelve aircraft took off at 10.56, the Marauders heading out over the Channel at 50 feet, maintaining 210 mph. Some thirty miles from the enemy coast, one of the aircraft experienced engine trouble; it climbed steeply and turned back, and as it did so it was picked up by the German radar. As the B-26s crossed the Dutch coast they were greeted by a storm of flak from the German coastal defences, now fully alerted. One B-26 was hit and broke sharply to port-right into the path of a second bomber. There was a blinding flash, and nothing remained of the two aircraft but a ball of debris. A third B-26 flew into the cloud of debris, rolled over and crashed on the beach. Stillman's aircraft had its controls shot away; upside down, it slammed into the sand dunes at 200 mph. Miraculously Stillman and one other crew member survived the crash and regained consciousness in a German hospital.

The two surviving aircraft of the first wave flew on towards the target, but in the general confusion they strayed into the defences of Amsterdam and were shot down. The five aircraft of the second wave meanwhile, their crews severely shaken by the loss of the aircraft ahead, were having trouble in getting their bearings. Lieutenant-Colonel Purinton was about to call off the mission and ask for a heading home when his navigator shouted that he had identified the target to the south-west. The

Marauders streaked towards Haarlem through heavy flak of all calibres. One of them was hit and made an emergency landing short of the town. The other three swept through the flak and dropped their bombs on the power station, then turned for the coast at 100 feet. As they flew over the dunes Lieutenant-Colonel Purinton's B-26 was badly damaged by flak. He managed to ditch half a mile offshore, where he and his crew were picked up by a German flak ship.

As the other three B-26s raced low over the sea they were attacked by three Messerschmitt 109s, which shot down two of them. The third, badly damaged, hit the sea and broke up. Two of the crew managed to get out and take to their dinghy; they were picked up four days later by a British ASR launch — the only survivors of the raid to come home. Twenty others spent the rest of the war in prison camps.

As a result of this disastrous attack it was decided that the B-26 was unsuitable for low-level attacks against strongly defended targets. Following additional training, all B-26 units in the European theatre were reassigned to the 8th Air Support Command in the medium-level role, which they fulfilled magnificently until the end of the war.

In June 1943 the Combined Chiefs of Staff issued their directive for the start of Operation Pointblank, the joint round-the-clock Anglo-American bombing offensive against Germany's war industries. In terms of offensive power the US 8th Air Force was well equipped to undertake such an operation: by the beginning of July its strength had increased to fifteen bomber groups comprising more than 300 B-17s and B-24S. The biggest obstacle to the success of deep-penetration daylight missions remained the lack of long-range fighter escort. In an effort to fill this critical gap the Americans slung drop-tanks under the wings of their Thunderbolts and Lightnings, which enabled them to penetrate as far as Germany's western frontier, but this did not provide a real solution. The first mission by Thunderbolts with drop-tanks, carried out on 28 July, was a success, but it was not long before the Focke-Wulf leaders developed new combat techniques that went a long way towards eliminating the Americans' advantage. The Focke-Wulfs would attack the Thunderbolts as they crossed the Dutch coast, forcing the P-47s to jettison their auxiliary tanks to increase manoeuvrability.

On 28 July the Thunderbolts escorted seventy-seven Fortresses in two formations as far as the German frontier before turning back. The bombers flew on towards their targets, the Fieseler works at Kassel-Bettenhausen and the AGO factories at Aschersleben, near Magdeburg. The *Luftwaffe* fighter *Gruppen* engaged the B-17S furiously from the moment they crossed the frontier, and one unit — II/JG 2 — employed a novel attack technique: its Messerschmitts flew at 3,000 feet over the bombers and dropped a shoal of 500-pound bombs on them. Three bombers in one formation were destroyed by this means. The remainder scattered wildly, and as they did so the Messerschmitts pounced. 11/JG 2 alone destroyed eleven bombers, and the total American loss was twenty-two. Several other bombers were badly damaged, four of them so seriously that they were written off in landing accidents on return to the UK.

During the last week of July the 8th Air Force made five major sorties against sixteen major targets. Their longest mission was a 1,900-mile flight to attack the German u-boat base at the Norwegian port of Trondheim, not far from the Arctic Circle. During seven days of operations the 8th Bomber Command lost eighty-eight aircraft, mostly Fortresses.

This intensive phase of air operations, which lasted for a full week, began with the Trondheim attack on 24 July. The next day the target was the Blohm und Voss shipyards at Hamburg, obscured by a pall of smoke from the massive fires started by RAF Bomber Command the night before. At the same time other formations attacked the shipyards at Kiel and the *Luftwaffe* training school and airfield at Wustrow. Nineteen B-17S failed to return.

On the 26th, the Fortresses struck at the Continental Gummiwerke A.G. at Hanover. They left the target in flames, with a massive mushroom of smoke rising to 20,000 feet. Sixteen bombers were shot down, and eight more were destroyed over Hamburg and other secondary targets.

On 27 July 8th Bomber Command stood down, its crews badly in need of a rest, but on the 28th the bombers began a three-day series of strikes against the German aircraft factories. Forty-four B-17S failed to return during this period; the loss would undoubtedly have been higher had it not been for the escort of Thunderbolts fitted with long-range tanks. The brunt of these bitter air battles was borne exclusively by the Fortresses.

Most of 8th Bomber Command's Liberator units had left for the Mediterranean to strike at Ploesti and other targets in southern Europe.

Then came August and the 'Anniversary Raids' of the 17th, when sixteen per cent of the bombers despatched failed to return. The disaster forced the 8th to conserve its strength for several weeks, during which attacks were carried out only against those targets within range of fighter cover. General Eaker, however, was determined to continue the long-range daylight offensive, and early in October the Americans were ready to resume their deep-penetration raids. When the attacks did start again, the lessons of August were rammed home even more forcibly. During one week between 8 and 14 October, when the Americans attacked Bremen, Marienburg, Danzig, Münster and once again Schweinfurt, they lost 148 bombers and nearly 1,500 aircrew. On the raid on Schweinfurt on 14 October, known as Black Thursday, the *Luftwaffe* flew over 500 sorties and destroyed sixty of the 280 bombers taking part — more than twenty per cent. Group Captain J. E. Johnson, leading a formation of Spitfires across the Channel to escort the bombers home, described the aftermath of this terrible encounter:

It was a clear afternoon, and we first saw their contrails many miles away, as well as the thinner darting contrails of the enemy fighters above and on either flank. As we closed the gap we could see that they had taken a terrible mauling, for there were gaping holes in their precise formations. Some Fortresses were gradually losing height, and a few stragglers, lagging well behind, were struggling to get home on three engines.

We swept well behind the stragglers and drove off a few 109s and 110s, but the great air battle was over, and what a fight it must have been, because more than half the bombers we nursed across the North Sea were shot up. One or two ditched in the sea, and many others, carrying dead and badly injured crew members, had to make crash-landings. How we longed for more drop tanks, so that some of the many hundreds of Spitfires based in Britain could play their part in the great battles over Germany ...

With the 8th Air Force reeling from this succession of disasters and RAF Bomber Command beginning to suffer increasingly heavy losses at the hands of the German night-fighter force, the prospect for the combined Allied air offensive looked grim. The need for a long-range escort fighter was now desperate. Fortunately for the Allies, such an aircraft was about to make its debut in the skies of Europe.

The aircraft was the p-51 Mustang, designed in 1940 by North American Aviation to meet an RAF requirement for a fast, heavily-armed fighter capable of operating effectively at heights of over 20,000 feet. The prototype made its maiden flight on 1 May 1941, and the British Direct Purchase Commission placed an order for 320. RAF test pilots reported that although the type showed excellent qualities as a low- and medium-altitude fighter, it was generally outclassed by the Spitfire v above 20,000 feet. It was therefore decided to use the Mustang as a high-speed ground attack and tactical reconnaissance fighter, and it was in this role that it entered service with Army Co-Operation Command in July 1942.

P-51s entered service with the USAAF in 1943, and the first Mustang unit arrived in Britain in November of that year. This was the 354th Fighter Group, equipped with P-51BS powered by Packard-built Rolls-Royce Merlin engines. Based at Boxted, near Colchester, the Group initially came under the command of the 9th Air Force. On 1 December the Group's P-51BS took off on their first operational mission — a sweep over Belgium and the Pas de Calais. The twenty-three pilots who took part were led by Lieutenant-Colonel Don Blakeslee of the Debden-based 4th Fighter Group, flying a p-47 Thunderbolt. On 5 December the 354th — now under the operational control of the 8th Air Force — flew the first p-51 mission to Amiens, but the *Luftwaffe* failed to appear and the Mustang pilots returned to base without having fired their guns in anger.

On 13 December the 354th flew the longest fighter mission of the war up to that date when the Mustangs — together with p-38 Lightnings of the 55th Fighter Group — escorted B-17S to Kiel and back, a round trip of 1,000 miles. Three days later, on the 16th, the Mustangs once again penetrated deep into Germany on an escort mission to Bremen, and it was on this raid that the Group's first enemy aircraft — a Bf 110 was destroyed, by Lieutenant Charles F. Gumm of the 355th Squadron.

By the end of the year the 354th had shot down eight enemy aircraft for the loss of eight Mustangs. It was a far from encouraging picture, and the pilots entered the new year determined to produce more favourable results. Their big chance came on 5 January 1944, when they once again escorted B-17S to Kiel. The American formation was attacked by shoals of Messerschmitt 110s and Focke-Wulf 190s and a savage dogfight developed. When it ended the Mustang pilots claimed the destruction of eighteen enemy aircraft for no loss. The *Luftwaffe* was also up in strength when the 354th escorted the Fortresses to Oschersleben on 11 January, and the Americans claimed nine enemy aircraft destroyed. On 11 February the Mustangs once again fought their way through strong enemy opposition to Frankfurt, claiming 14 enemy aircraft for the loss of two of their own number. In the last week of that month the Group undertook its deepest penetration mission so far — a 1,100-mile round trip to Leipzig. During this raid the Mustang pilots destroyed sixteen enemy fighters.

Even so one Mustang Group was not enough to bring about a dramatic reduction in the losses suffered by the heavy bombers, and in the first weeks of 1944 — with the 8th Air Force committed to the battle on a bigger scale than ever before — these once again assumed alarming proportions. Of the 238 bombers that struck at the fighter production factories at Oschersleben on 11 January, for example, 60 failed to return. But there was to be no respite: the top priority at the outset of 1944 was the destruction of the *Luftwaffe*, and it had to be achieved within a limited period as an essential prelude to the projected Allied invasion of Europe. 'Destroy the Enemy Air Force wherever you find them, in the air, on the ground and in the factories.' Such was the New Year directive that went out to all Commands from the USAAF Chief of Staff, General Arnold.

At the beginning of the year the Americans had established a new command structure for the conduct of strategic bombing in the European theatre. At its apex was HQ US Strategic Air Forces under the command of General Carl Spaatz, while new commanders were appointed to the Air Forces that were to bear the brunt of the offensive. In England Lieutenant-General James H. Doolittle took over command of the 8th Air Force from General Eaker, while the 15th Air Force in Italy was commanded by Major-General Nathan F. Twining. These two forces, with a thousand heavy bombers at their disposal, were assigned the task of carrying out Operation Argument — the destruction of the German aircraft industry, and particularly those factories engaged in fighter production.

There was no doubt that the task would be a formidable one, for the Luftwaffe's fighter strength had increased substantially during the winter months — and the first raid of Operation Argument, on 11 January, was proof enough that the *Luftwaffe* was capable of opposing the bombers with unprecedented ferocity. Undeterred, on 20 February the 8th Air Force launched what was at that time the biggest strategic air attack in history against several key aircraft factories in central Germany between Leipzig and Brunswick, with a massive armada of 941 bombers and 700 fighters crossing the Channel. The Americans had anticipated fierce opposition and correspondingly heavy losses, but although the *Luftwaffe* committed every available fighter to the battle the Allied fighter escort prevented a large proportion from getting through to the bombers. All the target factories were hit, some of them badly, and 21 Fortresses and Liberators failed to return.

It was an encouraging start to the ten days of non-stop air onslaught that was to become known as 'Big Week'. On the night of 20/21 February, the American daylight success was followed up by a raid by 600 Lancasters and Halifaxes of RAF Bomber Command on Stuttgart, another centre of aircraft production. As the returning RAF crews fell wearily into their beds in the dawn of 21 February, Fortresses and Liberators of the 8th Air Force were once again being readied for another attack on the aircraft factories at Brunswick. The following morning it was the turn of General Twining's 15th Air Force, which had been heavily committed to support of the landings at Anzio. While a strong force of Liberators and Fortresses set out to strike at the Messerschmitt aircraft factory at Regensburg from the south, the 8th Air Force again left their English bases to hit the factories in central Germany, as well as Gotha and Schweinfurt.

It was a bold attempt to crush the enemy defences between the jaws of a mighty pincer movement, but the mission was dogged by ill-luck right from the start. To begin with, the 8th's English bases were covered by a dense layer of cloud, and several bombers collided as they climbed up through it. The carefully laid plans for the assembly of the bomber force over eastern England were completely dislocated. Combat Wings were scattered all over the sky, and as a result two whole Bombardment Divisions — the 2nd and 3rd — were ordered to abort and return to their fields. Only the 1st Division set course over the Channel, and by this time the German coastal radar — which had been watching the movements of the wheeling mass of bombers on the other side for some time-had fully alerted the *Luftwaffe* fighter *Gruppen*.

As the bombers crossed the German frontier they were savagely attacked by over a hundred fighters of JG I and JG 2. The assault took the Americans completely by surprise. During previous attacks the Germans had concentrated their fighter defences in the immediate vicinity of the target, but this time they were attacking much further to the west. They found the bombers escorted by only a handful of Thunderbolts; the Mustangs were not due to rendezvous with the Fortresses until the latter were approaching the target area. What followed was a massacre. The fighters bored in again and again, and the burning wrecks of 44 Fortresses and Liberators lay scattered over a broad swathe of German territory from the Rhineland to the Harz Mountains. Only 99 out of the original force of 430 bombers that set out actually reached their primary targets, and only two of these targets were damaged. In the south the 15th Air Force units successfully attacked the Messerschmitt factory at Regensburg, but they were strongly opposed by the fighters of the *Luftwaffe's* 7th Air Division and fourteen bombers were shot down.

Bad weather brought a halt to strategic daylight operations for 48 hours. Then, on 24 February, 600 heavy bombers of the 8th and 15th Air Forces once again set out for Germany. The 15th's target was the Daimler-Benz aero-engine factories at Styria, in eastern Austria, and once again the bombers were strongly opposed by the 7th *Fliegerdivision*. Of the 87 Fortresses involved 17 — twenty per cent — failed to return. All 10 bombers in the rear box were destroyed, most of them by salvoes of air-to-air rockets fired by Messerschmitt 110s. The 8th Air Force's bomber stream, meanwhile — comprising 477 aircraft — was heading for its targets at Schweinfurt and Gotha. Both these objectives were badly hit, but the Americans lost another 44 aircraft. A third 8th Air Force wave struck at Tutow, Kreising and Posen, which were bombed against only minimal opposition. After dark Schweinfurt was again attacked by 700 Lancasters of RAF Bomber Command.

On 25 February favourable weather conditions extended over the whole of Germany, and the Strategic Air Forces launched over 800 bombers in a massive assault on the Messerschmitt factories at

Regensburg and Augsburg from south and west. As two bomber streams approached Regensburg from these different points of the compass, the officer commanding 7th *Fliegerdivision*, Major-General Huth, was faced with a difficult decision. He did not have enough fighters to deal with both enemy forces. The question was, which stream to concentrate on? In the end he decided to throw most of his *Gruppen* against the southern stream, consisting of 176 bombers. It was a wise choice: the Allied fighter escort was absent, and 33 bombers were shot down.

The bomber stream from the west, on the other hand, was considerably larger and was escorted by Mustangs. By this time three Mustang Groups were operational in Britain, and they soon began to make their presence felt. On this occasion comparatively few enemy fighters managed to break through the strong fighter screen. Those that did, together with the flak, accounted for 31 out of a total force of 738 Fortresses and Liberators. The overall loss of 64 heavy bombers during the day's operations was not light, but the damage they inflicted on the aircraft factories was enormous: at Regensburg the Messerschmitt works was practically levelled.

So ended 'Big Week', and — judging by the reconnaissance photographs that showed aircraft factories all over Germany in ruins — it had been a success. Initial reports that came in from the devastated factory areas too did nothing to dispel the confusion and despair that the Allied air offensive had caused in the *Luftwaffe* High Command and the Air Ministry. Immediate plans were made to salvage what was left of the fighter production resources, but at first there was little hope. At Regensburg the Messerschmitt factory was such a wasteland of ruins that salvage work seemed impossible, and the German Air Ministry was on the point of authorizing the erection of a factory on a different site when it received the first of a series of surprises. As workers dug into the rubble at Regensburg, they found that much of the factory's vital machinery was repairable and in some cases undamaged. The machine-tools were housed in new, hastily constructed workshops, and by the beginning of June the factory had regained its former output. As for the Messerschmitt factory at Augsburg, it needed only two weeks of round-the-clock work before production was back to normal. At an aircraft factory near Leipzig 160 crated fighters were salvaged from the ruins; almost all of them were found to be repairable. Under the direction of

Albert Speer, the minister of munitions and war production, factories were hastily dispersed to make it more difficult for the Allies to deliver another knock-out blow.

Although in the final analysis the 'Big Week' offensive made little difference to the output of single-seat fighters for the *Luftwaffe*, which reached the level of 2,000 per month by the middle of 1944, the daylight offensive of January-April 1944 cost the *Luftwaffe* more than a thousand pilots, many of them veteran Wing Commanders and Squadron Commanders. Although the claims of the Fortress and Liberator gunners were vastly inflated in the confusion of air battle, there was no escaping the fact that the *Luftwaffe* lost an average of fifty fighter pilots every time the Americans mounted a major raid. The Allied fighter escort, and particularly the Mustangs, began to account for more enemy aircraft with every passing week. On 6 March 1944 Mustangs appeared for the first time in the sky over Berlin and took part in one of the most bitterly contested air battles of the war. For hours a raging battle was fought between 200 German fighters and 660 heavy bombers and their escort. When it ended the Americans had lost 69 bombers and 11 fighters, but the Germans lost 80 aircraft — almost half the defending force.

During March 1944 one Mustang Group-the 4th-alone claimed 156 enemy aircraft destroyed, and as the month wore on the German defences became noticeably weaker. Another attack on Berlin by 590 bombers and 801 fighters on 8 March, when several key factories were destroyed, cost the Americans 37 bombers and 17 fighters — but when 669 bombers again struck at the German capital on the 22nd they encountered almost no opposition. Twelve bombers were shot down, but all of them were victims of the flak.

In the south too the *Luftwaffe* was being steadily decimated. On 16 March a force of heavy bombers sent out to attack Augsburg was intercepted by 43 twin-engined Messerschmitt 110s of *Zerstorer-Geschwader* 76. Their rockets accounted for five bombers, but then the Mustang escort pounced and 26 110s went down in flames. For Messerschmitt's elderly 'Destroyer', which had fought its way through the war from the beginning in Poland, it was the end. It was withdrawn from the air defence role and replaced by the more modern Messerschmitt 410.

The great offensive continued, with the Allies now virtual masters of the daylight sky over Germany. Throughout April 1944 priority was still given to attacks on the enemy's aircraft industry. Then, in May, the offensive was switched to oil, synthetic fuel and hydrogen plants. On 12 May a mighty armada of 935 heavy bombers and 1,000 fighters struck at the synthetic oil plants of Brüx, Bohlen, Leuna, Zwickau and Lützendorf. In spite of suicidal attacks by a few German fighter *Gruppen*, most got through and delivered beautiful precision attacks. The plant at Brüx was completely wiped out, and production of the others cut back by as much as sixty per cent. Meanwhile the Italian-based 15th Air force hit the Rumanian oilfields and refineries twenty times in six weeks.

Day after day in that fateful spring and early summer of 1944 the solid phalanxes of bombers dragged their vapour trails over the shattered cities of the Third Reich, selecting their targets almost at will. The dwindling band of *Luftwaffe* fighter pilots fought them with desperate courage, but against the swarms of Mustangs and Thunderbolts courage was not enough. The *Luftwaffe* was sliding rapidly towards a crushing defeat, a defeat inflicted not by the bombing of its resources on the ground, but by the daily struggle against murderous odds high above the earth.

5 - Mediterranean Victory

'First of all you must win the battle of the air. That must come before you start a single sea or land engagement. If you examine the conduct of my campaigns, you will find that we never fought a land battle until the air battle was won.'

So spoke Field Marshal Montgomery in December 1943, referring to the successful Allied campaigns of 1942-3 in North Africa — the prelude to the invasion of Sicily. The initial object of these campaigns had been to defend the Suez Canal and the Anglo-Persian oilfields. When this had been achieved the goal was widened to include the elimination of the Axis forces in North Africa and the capture of the entire southern shore of the Mediterranean. By May 1943 the last pockets of Axis resistance in Tunisia had been wiped out, and Rommel's once proud Afrika Korps had ceased to exist. Vast Allied land and air forces now stood idle in North Africa, and the question of their future employment became a matter of urgent priority. With no prospect of launching an invasion of Occupied Europe across the Channel in 1943, there remained two alternatives: either the forces in North Africa could be transferred to Burma and the Pacific to take part in the war against Japan, or they could follow up their African victory by invading Sicily and Italy. In the latter event the objective would be to eliminate Italy from the war and open the road for an Allied advance into Austria and beyond, with the possibility of liberating Yugoslavia, Hungary and Czechoslovakia. This was the course that was chosen by the Allied leaders. It was an important decision, for the capture of Italian airfields would bring targets in south-east Germany within range of the North Africa-based heavy bombers of the 15th US Air Force.

During 1942, with the USAAF in Europe still gathering its forces for the coming daylight assault on Germany and RAF Bomber Command heavily committed in the west, the Allied strategic bombing effort in the Mediterranean theatre was strictly limited. Although detachments of UK-based Wellingtons and Halifaxes operated from Malta and Egypt on a rotation basis and made frequent attacks on the Italian mainland, the air war in the Middle East was by its very nature a tactical operation, and it was not until September 1942 that a heavy four-engined bomber unit was permanently stationed in the theatre. This was No. 462 Squadron RAF, which was formed by detachments of Nos 10, 76 and 227 Squadrons.

What was to become a massive American strategic bombing commitment in the Middle East had its beginning on 12 June 1942, when 13 B-24 Liberators of a detachment operating from Egypt bombed the Ploesti oilfields in Rumania. The first USAAF attack on Italy was carried out on 4 December, when B-24S raided Naples harbour. At the end of 1942 the Allied long-range bomber units in the Mediterranean were grouped within the framework of the North-west African Strategic Air Force, commanded by General J. H. Doolittle. On one occasion Doolittle — who gained fame in April 1942 by leading a formation of 16 North American B-25s which flew from the carrier USS *Hornet* to make a low-level attack on Tokyo — flew in a Wellington of No. 142 Squadron RAF to observe at first hand the result of a raid against Alghero in Sardinia.

By February 1943 the North-west African Strategic Air Force, now having the status of a command within the North-west African Air Forces under General Carl Spaatz, comprised two Bombardment Wings of the US 15th Air Force and Wellington and Halifax squadrons of No. 205 Group RAF. The following June all bomber units took part in a massive twenty-day air assault on the island of Pantellaria as a prelude to its occupation by the Allies. The latter encountered little resistance: what had been a heavily defended objective had been completely overwhelmed by air power.

The stage was now set for the invasion of Sicily. As a preliminary to the airborne and seaborne assault the enemy airfields on the island were subjected to an intense bombardment by heavy and medium bombers of the RAF, SAAF and USAAF, with Malta-based Spitfires, Beaufighters and Mosquitoes providing cover. The actual landings were to begin with a glider assault by airborne troops and a parachute drop by the 82nd Airborne Division of the US 7th Army, and to support the operation the Allies had mustered 670 first-line aircraft on the islands of Malta, Gozo and Pantellaria and on the Cap Bon Peninsula of Tunisia.

Despite a series of initial setbacks the conquest of the island went ahead, and as the former enemy airfields on Sicily fell into Allied hands one by one the British and American squadrons began to move in. Apart from close support operations the land offensive was supported by strategic bombing attacks on targets in Italy. On the night of 12/13 July Lancasters of No. 5 Group from the UK attacked Turin in an effort to disrupt rail communications between southern Italy and north-west Europe, from where German reinforcements were already racing to the Mediterranean theatre. Thirteen Lancasters failed to return from this mission. Two days later about 200 Fortresses, Marauders and Mitchells, escorted by Lockheed p-38 Lightnings, attacked the docks area and marshalling yards at Messina, and on the 15th RAF Wellingtons and USAAF Fortresses raided docks, railways and industrial areas in and around Naples. Allied bombing reached a peak of intensity on 17 July, when over 500 aircraft attacked Naples and targets in the surrounding area. The raids began before dawn with an attack by Wellingtons, which were followed after daybreak by Mitchells, Fortresses and Liberators.

Meanwhile, as the Allies consolidated their positions in Sicily and prepared to thrust across the Straits of Messina to gain a foothold on the Italian mainland, plans were being laid for a strategic bombing attack which, it was hoped, would deal a crippling blow to the German war effort. The target was the Ploesti oil refineries near Bucharest, which supplied the bulk of the Axis' oil and petrol. Five Bomb Groups of the US 9th Air Force — the 44th, 93rd, 98th, 376th and 389th-were to take part in the mission, flying from North African bases. The attack was to be made at roof-top level in the hope of taking the enemy defences completely by surprise.

At 07.10 on 1 August the first B-24 Liberator of the lead Group-the 376th, under Colonel Keith K. Compton-took off from an airfield near Benghazi, and thirty minutes later 177 Liberators were airborne. A 178th aircraft, belonging to the 98th Group, crashed on take-off and exploded, killing all its crew. Eleven more aircraft aborted for various reasons during the minutes that followed.

Then, ninety minutes after take-off, came the first incident in a chain of circumstances that was to turn the mission into a tragic fiasco. Without warning and for no apparent reason the leading aircraft of the 376th Group — carrying the Group Navigation Officer, Captain Anderson — suddenly stalled and spun into the sea. The other Liberators began to straggle, their pilots confused as to who should take over the lead, and because of the strict radio silence there was no way of passing the necessary information. In the end Colonel Compton's Liberator, which was also carrying General Ent, chief of the 9th Air Force Bomber Command, moved into the lead position. Because of the relative inexperience of Compton's navigator, Compton and General Ent assumed the navigation task for the Group.

At 12.20, as the Liberators crossed Albania and were approaching Yugoslavia, they began to run into cloud, and the carefully planned tight formation — designed to afford the maximum defensive firepower — became dislocated as the Groups lost sight of one another. The two leading Groups, the 376th and 93rd, crossed the Rumanian frontier on schedule and set course for their first turning point — Pitesti, some sixty miles west of Ploesti — but the three Groups that followed lost valuable time as they circled over the Danube, trying to get into some sort of order. When they finally set course they were twenty minutes late.

The 376th and 93rd Groups, meanwhile, roared across the Rumanian landscape at 200 feet. As they flashed past Pitesti they came down even lower, leapfrogging trees and houses at a height of only thirty feet. The crews retained vivid impressions of startled farmworkers in the fields. Some hurled themselves flat, while others stood their ground and threw pitchforks at the speeding aircraft.

From Pitesti the Liberators were to steer due east, past Targoviste and on to Floresti. From there they were to turn south-east and follow the railway line to Ploesti. This route would enable them to approach the refinery from the north, and each crew had been briefed to pick out its individual target from this direction. When the two leading Groups reached Targoviste, however, they sighted a railway leading south — and Compton and Ent decided that this was their turning point. Compton's young navigator protested that it was a mistake, but he was overridden by the general. So Compton's Liberator and sixty other aircraft turned to follow the line — which led not to Ploesti but to Bucharest. It was only when the spires of the Rumanian capital showed up ahead that Compton and Ent realized their mistake, but by then it was too late. The enemy flak batteries were alerted and Focke-Wulfs and Messerschmitts were taking off from every fighter airfield in the Balkans. Realizing that it was now futile to maintain radio silence, Ent told the other crews that he was making a left turn towards Ploesti. This would bring them up against the southern edge of the refinery area, an approach angle on which none of them had been briefed.

The three remaining Groups, meanwhile, had reached Pitesti. As the 389th broke to port to make an individual attack on the refineries at Campina, fifteen miles north-west of Ploesti, the others flew on to Floresti and correctly turned on track for the target area. As they approached from the north, the 376th and 93rd Groups were sweeping in on a converging course from the south, running the gauntlet of intense flak. The German gunners fired point-blank over open sights, directly into the path of the bombers. The 376th Group was the first to approach the target, and Compton led his aircraft round in a wide twenty-mile semicircle to try and arrive over Ploesti from the correct angle. The flak, however, was even more intense on this approach lane, and Ent — aware at last that the carefully laid plan of attack would have to be abandoned — directed the crews to attack targets of opportunity. One squadron selected the Concordia Vega plant and bombed it successfully, emerging from the pall of smoke with their aircraft covered in soot. This target had in fact been

reserved for the 93rd Group, which had chosen to go straight in from the south. Not more than five aircraft succeeded in bombing the primary target; the rest dropped their loads more or less at random over a wide area. The Liberator carrying the 93rd's commander, Lieutenant-Colonel Addison Baker, was shot down seconds after releasing its bombs; ten more aircraft of the Group were destroyed over the target, one crashing into a women's prison.

Meanwhile the 44th Group under Colonel Leon Johnson and the 98th led by Colonel John Kane were entering the target area from the north. The Group commanders had no idea of the seriousness of the blunders that had been made until they saw several Liberators of the 376th Group flash past beneath them heading south-west, and observed that several of the targets earmarked for attack by the 44th and 98th had already been bombed. This meant that both Groups had to fly directly into a holocaust of smoke and flame, running the risk of being destroyed in the explosions of delayed-action bombs. There was no alternative: the Liberators bored in, racing through towers of flame rising to 300 feet and more. The huge bombers were tossed like corks in the fearsome turbulence. Several were unable to recover and dived into the ground, others were incinerated in vast explosions. 'We all felt sick when we saw the oil tanks exploding,' commented one of the pilots who survived. 'Somebody ahead had bombed our target by mistake. There was nothing to do but try and hit it again; there was no time for another run on this trip.'

Conditions over the Campina refinery, the target assigned to Colonel Jack Wood's 389th Group, were little better. The flak was murderous, and although the target was hit accurately several Liberators were destroyed. A few minutes later Campina was also bombed by some Liberators of the 376th Group, searching for a target of opportunity.

As the scattered Liberators turned away from the Ploesti target area, the first of the enemy fighters pounced. They had been circling overhead, clear of the terrific flak barrage, waiting their opportunity. Just about every Axis fighter type was represented: German Messerschmitts and Focke-Wulfs, Italian Fiats and Macchis, Rumanian IAR 81s-even a few biplanes identified as Gloster Gladiators by the American crews, although in reality probably Fiat CR.42s. At first the bombers were comparatively safe from air attack. As long as they stayed at low level the enemy fighters found it difficult to engage them, but as soon as they climbed to cross the mountains the slaughter began. One by one the B-24S went down in flames; stragglers had no chance of escape. Precious fuel was used up as the American pilots manoeuvred desperately to avoid the determined fighter attacks, with the result that few of the survivors managed to regain North Africa. Some limped into Cyprus and Sicily; others made emergency landings in Turkey. The fearful cost of failure was more than fifty heavy bombers, with 440 airmen killed or missing, 200 prisoners of war and many more wounded.

This disaster brought an effective halt to deep-penetration daylight missions over southern Europe by the USAAF until long-range escort fighters became available early in 1944, and for the next few months the American heavy bombers in the Mediterranean theatre were employed mainly in support of the Allied offensive in Italy, which was invaded on 3 September. The RAF'S heavy bombers, on the other hand, continued to range across the Balkans under cover of darkness. In addition to strategic bombing many minelaying operations were carried out in enemy waters — notably in the Danube, a key enemy supply route.

Late in 1943 the North-west African Strategic Air Force turned its attention to targets in southern France, the American daylight bombers attacking the naval base at Toulon and submarine pens and construction works in Marseille harbour. In the middle of December the air offensive was carried to airfields and shipping near Athens; the air bases at Eleusis, Kalamaki and Tatoi were all badly damaged, as was the harbour at Piraeus. On 20 December B-17S and B-24S operating from Italy attacked Augsburg and Innsbruck in southern Germany, the railway yards at Augsburg being badly hit.

At the beginning of 1944 long-range daylight missions over the Balkans once again became a matter of routine, the Fortress and Liberator formations now escorted by P-38 Lightning, p-47 Thunderbolt or p-51 Mustang fighters. One of the main strategic aims of the US 15th Air Force during this phase was to inflict as much damage as possible on that portion of the enemy's air power which could be brought to bear on the Italian war zone. Another aim was to delay the arrival of troop reinforcements from the Balkans. To this end Sofia was heavily bombed six times in two months, the Bulgarian capital being the hub of the German-controlled supply system for all south-eastern Europe. On 16 January Fortresses struck for the first time against the Messerschmitt aircraft factory at Klagenfurt, lying in the Carinthian Alps some 14 miles from the Yugoslav border. On the 30th the 15th Air Force attacked airfields in north-east Italy from which enemy bombers arriving from the Balkans refuelled before taking off to bomb the Allied concentrations in the Anzio and Nettuno bridgeheads.

By this time the heavy bombers of the 15th Air Force were concentrated on airfields around Foggia, in southern Italy, which brought them within easy range of many major targets which it had hitherto been impossible to attack. Nevertheless it was some time before the strategic air offensive from Italy got into its full stride. It took a considerable time to build up at Foggia all the supplies and facilities necessary for the operation of a heavy bomber force, and during the winter of 1943-4 the weather over Italy was abysmal. With improved conditions in the spring, however, the Allied bombers renewed their day and night offensive against the enemy's oil resources in the Balkans — and this time it was not long before the mastery of the Balkan sky which the enemy fighters had enjoyed in 1943 was wrested from them.

In the Mediterranean theatre there were four us Fighter Groups equipped with P-51 Mustangs: the 52nd (12th Air Force) and the 31st, 325th and 332nd (15th Air Force). In the spring of 1944 all four Groups — which had been operating intensively in the tactical role in support of the land campaign in Italy — were assigned to long-range escort as a primary task.

On 21 April 1944 the 31st Fighter Group mounted its first 'big show' with the new Mustangs when it was detailed to escort a B-24 mission raiding the oil refineries at Ploesti. The Group's task was to meet the bombers after they had left the target area and shepherd them home. Near Bucharest the Mustang pilots sighted a formation of B-24S being attacked by at least sixty enemy fighters. Attacking out of the sun, the Americans took the enemy completely by surprise and a savage dogfight sprang up. Two Mustangs went down in flames, but the 31st's pilots claimed 17 enemy fighters destroyed, 7 probably destroyed and 10 damaged. It was a notable success which earned the Group a Distinguished Unit Citation.

On 22 July, the 31st Fighter Group was once again detailed for an escort mission to Ploesti. While bomb-carrying p-38 Lightnings of the 82nd Group attacked the oil refinery installations, the Mustangs strafed a nearby airfield before going on to land at Piryatin in Russia. On 25 July 35 Mustangs escorted the P-38s on a ground-attack mission to the German airfield at Mielec in Poland. During the return flight they ran headlong into a formation of 36 Junkers and 87 Stukas, laden with bombs and heading for the Russian lines. The Mustangs ripped in among the slow-flying dive bombers and a frightful slaughter ensued. Within minutes the wreckage of 27 Stukas was blazing on the ground. This destruction of an entire *Luftwaffe* dive-bomber Wing earned the 31st Group its second Distinguished Unit Citation. On 26th July the Mustangs flew back to their bases in Italy.

The use of Russian airfields by Allied aircraft resulted from an operational plan known as Project Frantic, designed to enable us bombers to strike at targets which had previously been out of range. The bombers, operating out of Britain or bases in Italy, would bomb selected targets on the outward trip, land in Russia to refuel and rearm, then strike at other targets on their way home. As a secondary aim, it was hoped that these 'shuttle-bombing' operations would force the *Luftwaffe* to disperse its already overstretched resources still further in an effort to meet the new attacks over a larger strategic area made up of German-held Polish territory.

Negotiations began in December 1943, but it was not until the following April that the Russians finally agreed to the use of their bases by the American bombers — and even then they allocated only three airfields instead of the six required. All three airfields lay in the devastated 'scorched earth' area around Kiev, and throughout April and May 1944 hordes of American engineers worked hard to extend runways, build new base facilities and generally get the fields into shape. Of the three, only Poltava was really suitable for handling heavy bombers; Mirgorod could accommodate only a few, while Piryatin was just big enough to be used by fighters.

Project Frantic was finally launched on 2 June 1944, when 30 B-17S and 70 p-51 Mustangs of the 15th Air Force took off from their Italian bases, bombed the marshalling yards at Debrecen and flew on to the airfields in Russia. From there, on 6 June, they struck at the airfield of Galatz in Rumania; and on the 11th, on their way back to Italy, they also bombed the Rumanian airfield at Foscani. Only two B-17S and two Mustangs were lost in the three operations.

On 21 June it was the turn of the 8th Air Force, based in Britain. During the early part of June the 8th AAF — like all Allied strategic bombing forces in the UK — had been totally committed to tactical operations in support of the Normandy landings, but by the middle of the month the situation on the ground was well under control and strategic attacks on targets deep inside Germany were resumed. On the 21st a vast force of 2,500 American bombers and fighters was despatched to attack various objectives in Germany and Occupied Europe. One of the principal targets was Berlin, and as the main force approached the enemy capital a smaller group of 114 B-17S and 70 P-5 is broke away and bombed a synthetic oil plant at Ruhland, seventy-five miles further south. This force then flew on towards the 'Frantic' airfields around Kiev, which were reached late that afternoon. Seventy-five of the B-17S landed at Poltava; the rest touched down at Mirgorod, while the Mustangs assembled at Piryatin.

What the American crews did not know was that, as they droned high over eastern Europe, they had been shadowed by a lone Heinkel 177 long-range bomber. As darkness fell eighty Junkers 88s and Heinkel 111s of General Rudolf Meister's iv Fliegerkorps took off from airfields behind the German lines and headed east. Before long the Americans were to learn to their cost that the *Luftwaffe* was still capable of striking fast and hard.

At 23.35 Russian authorities warned the American HQ staff at Poltava that enemy aircraft had crossed the front line and were reported to be heading for the Kiev area. The alert was sounded and the Allied personnel on the three 'Frantic' airfields took cover. Thirty minutes passed; nothing happened, and the tension began to ease a little. Then, a few minutes after midnight, there was a sudden roar of engines in the darkened sky over Poltava and clusters of brilliant flares cascaded down on the airfield, dropped by Heinkel HIS of Kampfgeschwader 4. The Flying Fortresses, only one of which was camouflaged, stood out vividly in the garish light. More flares were dropped during the next ten minutes. The Russian anti-aircraft batteries put up a furious barrage but failed to hit anything. Then the first bombs fell. For an hour Poltava was pounded incessantly by the He HIS and Ju 88s of KGS 27, 53 and 55, the aircraft bombing singly from altitudes up to 10,000 feet. The last wave, consisting entirely of Ju 88s, swept over the field at low level, raking it with cannon and machine-gun fire.

When the last of the bombers droned away, they left the airfield at Poltava littered with the burning wrecks of 47 B-17S, and every one of the twenty-six remaining bombers had suffered damage. Several Russian and American fighters and two c-47 transports had also been destroyed. Nearly half a million gallons of petrol had gone up in flames. Thirty Russians and two Americans had been killed, while a hundred Allied personnel had been wounded. The enemy bombers had dropped a total of 110 tons of bombs, of which 15 tons were high explosive, 78 tons antipersonnel and 17 tons incendiary. Not a single German aircraft had been lost. The Poltava disaster, taken together with the casualties suffered by the 8th AAF'S Bomber Command in action over Germany earlier that day, represented an overall loss of ninety-one aircraft — the highest ever sustained by the Americans in a single operation.

Twenty-four hours later the *Luftwaffe* tried to repeat this success in an attack on Mirgorod, but by that time the Americans had gone. Never again would the *Luftwaffe* achieve so much in a single blow. The creation of a long-range bomber force on the Eastern Front had come too late, and the long withdrawal that took place during the following months effectively took most important Russian strategic targets outs of range of the German aircraft. As for Operation Frantic, the shuttle-bombing tactics continued on and off for the next two months before being dropped for good.

The war in Italy, meanwhile, dragged on. For a time in March it had been touch and go for the Allies. General Kesselring threw all his resources into a third major offensive against the Anzio beachhead, and after thirty-six hours of bitter fighting had begun to make substantial headway when the Allies turned the whole weight of their tactical and strategic air power in the Mediterranean against the enemy positions. Forty thousand fragmentation bombs were dropped by heavy bombers alone on troop concentrations and supply dumps in and around Cisterna, Carroceto and Campo Leone, while fighters and fighter-bombers attacked enemy transport around Albano, Frascati and west of Valmonte.

Similar measures were applied, although not with as much success, against Cassino, where the Allied advance had ground to a halt against strong enemy defences. On 15 March 1944 more than 1,400 tons of bombs were dropped on the town, reducing it to rubble. But the bombing defeated its own object. The resulting devastation impeded the subsequent progress of Allied tanks, and the defenders — German paratroops, who had taken refuge in catacombs beneath the town and the ancient monastery during the air attack — were able to resist ferociously from strongpoints among the ruins.

In April 1944 the Allied Strategic Air Forces began an intensive assault on targets along the Mediterranean coast of France. Between 28 April and 10 August they flew no fewer than 10,000 missions, dropping 12,000 tons of bombs. One of the primary aims was to destroy the enemy's naval facilities, principally his u-boat capability, before the invasion of southern France — which was scheduled to take place some six weeks after the thrust across the English Channel into Normandy. On 6 August 360 tons of bombs went down on the fortifications of Toulon and the strategic Saint-Mandrier Peninsula during an eight-hour raid aimed at the docks, port facilities and submarine pens. In this devastating attack the heavy bombers sank four out of the eight submarines assigned to the

Kriegsmarine's 29th Fleet, as well as two tugboats and a submarine chaser.

The total number of Allied aircraft based in the Mediterranean theatre was 5,000, over half of which were assembled on Corsica and Sardinia. For two weeks beginning on 1 August massive formations of four-engined bombers winging northwards across the Mediterranean became a familiar sight as the 12th and 15th Air Forces took turns to strike at targets in France and northern Italy from dawn to dusk. The air attacks lasted until 03.30 on Tuesday, 15 August 1944. It had been agreed that the bombings should start fairly early, but they were combined into a wider overall programme designed to inflict extensive damage in the area where the seaborne landings were to take place. The strategic preparation for the landings in Provence consequently began with attacks on targets in the Rhone Valley, to prevent German reinforcements from reaching the invasion front. Air bases in Italy, in Udine and in the Po Valley, as well as in southern France, were also attacked to whittle away the Luftwaffe's power of resistance. On 7 August 300 heavy bombers flying in close formation laid a carpet of bombs on targets between Nice and Montpellier, returning the next day to attack Imperia and the Italian Riviera. On 10 August 510 Mitchell and Marauder medium bombers struck at the rear of the German armies retreating towards Florence, leading Field Marshal Kesselring to believe that an Allied landing was imminent between Genoa and San Remo and putting the enemy defences along this part of the coast in a state of alert. The following day 12th and 15th Air Force bombers and fighter-bombers attacked over radar stations on the Mediterranean coast, completely destroying the large installations at La Ciotat, Mont-Rose and Cap Camarat, near Saint-Tropez.

The final phase of 'Operation Nutmeg', the softening-up of the enemy-held Mediterranean coast by the Strategic Air Forces, began on Monday 14 August. On that date the enemy coastal radar stations were again attacked, while aircraft of the 47th Bombardment Group subjected the Luftwaffe's bases to yet another intense bombardment. After nightfall the RAF'S Halifaxes and Wellingtons pounded the port of Marseille, while Liberators of the 12th Air Force hit Genoa and targets in the surrounding area. All along a 45-mile stretch of coast, Allied aircraft hammered the beaches and the installations behind them.

At dawn on 15 August, under a pall of smoke caused by the previous day's bombing, the first Allied troops stormed ashore between Cape Benat and St Raphael. Victory in the Mediterranean was now assured, and the ring of steel around the Third Reich was closing fast.

6 - Confound and Destroy - No. 100 Group, 1943-5

The introduction of 'Window' on Bomber Command operations in July 1943 threw the German air defences into temporary confusion, and was accompanied by a corresponding drop in the RAF'S casualty figures. Nevertheless it was not long before the enemy regained some of their earlier initiative, thanks mainly to Major Hajo Herrmann's *Wilde Sau* tactics, involving the use of large numbers of single-engined Focke-Wulf 190s on free-lance night-fighter operations independently of the jammed air-defence control system. In the autumn of 1943 Bomber Command's loss rate had once again risen to eighty per cent of the level it had reached prior to the use of Window.

Furthermore British Intelligence was aware that the Germans were working hard to develop countermeasures against Window, and that a new AI radar — the Lichtenstein SN-2, which worked on a frequency of 90 megacycles and was consequently free from both electronic and Window jamming — was in full production. It was therefore likely to be only a question of time before Bomber Command's casualty figures took an even more alarming turn for the worse.

To combat the renewed menace, a higher degree of priority was given to the development of more advanced radio countermeasures equipment, and on 8 November 1943 the Air Ministry issued an Establishment Directive making provision for the formation of a special countermeasures Group — No. 100. The Group's task was defined as follows:

a. To give direct support to night bombing or other operations by attack of enemy night-fighter aircraft in the air, or by attack of ground installations.

b. To employ airborne and ground radio countermeasures equipment to deceive or jam enemy radio navigational aids, enemy radar systems and certain wireless signals.

c. To examine all intelligence on the offensive and defensive radar, radio navigation, and signalling systems of the enemy, with a view to future action within the scope of (a) and (b).

d. From the examination of this intelligence, to plan for use in future operations means of disorganizing the enemy offensive and defensive radio systems.

e. To provide immediate information, additional to normal intelligence information, as to the movements and employment of enemy fighter aircraft to enable the tactics of the bomber force to be immediately notified to meet any changes.

*

The officer selected to command No. 100 Group was Air Vice-Marshal E. B. Addison, who in 1940-1 had been in charge of the RAF'S 'Ruffian' operations designed to disrupt the enemy's radio navigation beams. Since then he had played a leading part in directing the British radio countermeasures effort. His headquarters as AOG 100 Group was initially at West Raynham; at a later date it was moved to Bylaugh Hall, an old mansion not far from Dereham.

No. 100 Group's early establishment consisted of three squadrons transferred from Fighter Command: Nos 141, 169 and 239. It was some time before the last two became fully operational in their new role, as both had been operating Mustangs and it was now necessary for them to be re-equipped with Mosquito night-fighters. No. 141 Squadron, however, had been operating Beaufighters in the airborne interception role for some time, and its crews had considerable experience of night-fighter tactics. Their aircraft were equipped with 'Serrate', a homing device developed by the Telecommunications Research Establishment and designed to enable the night-fighters to home on to the enemy's Lichtenstein AI transmissions. The range of Serrate varied between 50 miles when the Lichtenstein was pointed towards it and 10 miles when it was pointing away. It was first used operationally in June 1943, and with its help No. 141 scored twenty-three kills during the next three months.

Normal AI radar was used in the final stages of interception, and on several occasions German night-fighters came under attack as they themselves were engaged in attacking RAF bombers.

The Mosquito crews of Nos 169 and 239 Squadrons, on the other hand, had no experience of Serrate operations. Moreover the Mosquito 11 aircraft with which they were initially equipped were worn out and their operations had to be severely curtailed so that they could be re-engined with new Rolls-Royce Merlin 22s. These factors all contributed to the initial low success rate of 100 Group's long-range fighter arm. During their first three months of operations the three squadrons combined claimed only 31 enemy aircraft destroyed or damaged, and of these 6 fell to the guns of one pilot: Wing Commander Bob Braham, flying a Mosquito. In March 1944 No. 100 Group's fighter force was joined by No. 515 Squadron, operating Beaufighters and later Mosquito vis. This unit, however, was used for intruder operations and was not equipped with Serrate.

Several problems too were experienced in the creation of 100 Group's radio countermeasures force. The first lay in the choice of a suitable aircraft. To carry the necessary jamming equipment it had to be large, which ruled out the Mosquito, and it had to be able to fly high enough and fast enough to stand a chance of evading enemy night-fighters, which would have little difficulty in homing on to its continual radio jamming transmissions. This in turn eliminated the Lancaster and Halifax. The aircraft finally selected was the American B-17 Fortress, which — because of its size, its ability to cruise at 28,000 feet and its heavy defensive armament of ten .5 machine-guns — was considered to meet all the requirements. Fourteen B-17FS were obtained, and necessary modifications were carried out early in 1944 by the Scottish Aviation Company at Prestwick. These included the replacement of the Fortress's chin turret by an H2S blister, the provision of mufflers to screen the exhaust flames, and the fitting of the jamming devices themselves in the bomb-bay.

There were three principal types of jammer. The first was 'Mandrel', a radar jammer developed at the Wembley laboratories of the General Electric Company. Each aircraft carried eight Mandrel transmitters; operating in pairs, they were capable of jamming the whole enemy early warning frequency from 88 to 200 megacycles. The second device was 'Piperack', developed from Mandrel to cover the 90-110 megacycles frequency used by the German airborne interception radars. Aircraft fitted with this equipment carried six transmitters; these were sufficient to cover half the enemy waveband, so the machines normally operated in pairs. The third device was 'Jostle', which emitted a high-pitched wail on 38-42 megacycles VHF and 3-6 megacycles HF, the German Fighter Control frequencies. Each aircraft carried one Jostle in place of its ventral gun turret.

The countermeasures Fortresses began operations with No. 214 Squadron RAF in April 1944. In addition aircraft of the 803rd Squadron, United States Strategic Air Forces, were also fitted for the jamming role, and this unit was placed under the operational control of 100 Group. In their finalized form, the tactics used were as follows: Mandrel-equipped aircraft, employed mainly to provide a screen for the main bomber force, would operate in pairs with 14 miles between them, forming a line position some 80 miles from enemy-occupied territory. With their Mandrels switched on, the orbiting aircraft formed an effective electronic 'curtain' through which the enemy search radars were unable to penetrate. Aircraft equipped with Jostle and Piperack, on the other hand, flew 4,000 feet above the main bomber stream at intervals of 10 miles, providing an electronic umbrella to disrupt the German AI radar and voice communications.

No. 100 Group aircraft also made extensive use of Window in support of their radio jamming. A Window 'spoof' usually consisted of 24 aircraft, flying in two lines of 12 machines with 2 ½ miles between each one, the lines separated by a distance of 30 miles. Two bundles of Window were dropped from each aircraft at minute intervals, enabling the formation to provide blanket coverage over an area 60 miles long by 20 miles wide — an area similar to that covered by an actual raid of 500 bombers. In conjunction with the spoof, aircraft of the main force also discharged bundles of Window at intervals of ten minutes, so that the spoof and the attacking force appeared as identical echoes on the enemy radar screens.

The strength of 100 Group's jamming force was substantially increased in the summer of 1944, when the Fortresses of 214 Squadron were joined by the Liberators of No. 223. Together these two squadrons assumed the main responsibility for jamming with the aid of Jostle and Piperack. The Mandrel operations, which did not require fast high-flying aircraft since they always took place well clear of enemy territory, were taken over by the Stirlings of No. 199 Squadron and the Halifaxes of No. 171. They were joined at the end of 1944 by the Halifaxes of No. 642 Squadron.

Earlier in the year, meanwhile, Sir Arthur Harris had been making determined efforts to persuade the Air Staff to give priority to the allocation of more night-fighter squadrons to 100 Group. In April he wrote a strong letter to the Vice-Chief of the Air Staff in which he recommended the transfer of at least ten fighter squadrons to the Group. In the event, a conference summoned at the Air Ministry on the 20th of that month decided to authorize the transfer of only three. These were Nos 85 and 157, equipped with Mosquitoes, and No. 515. Shortly after joining the Group, the latter unit also exchanged its Beaufighters for Mosquitoes.

This meagre increase did little to improve the effectiveness of 100 Group's night-fighter force. One of the problems was that Mosquitoes equipped with the latest Mk II AI radar were forbidden to operate over enemy territory, and the earlier Mk iv that equipped most of the 100 Group night-fighters was subjected to increasing interference from enemy countermeasures. To make matters worse, the usefulness of Serrate was over. The Lichtenstein AI radar on which it was designed to home had now been replaced by the more advanced SN-2, which worked outside Serrate's frequency cover. The end result was frustration for the night-fighter crews. In June 1944, for example, only one enemy aircraft was destroyed in the course of 140 sorties. The situation improved somewhat towards the end of 1944, when Mosquitoes equipped with the latest marks of AI radar were cleared to operate over enemy territory and the old Serrate Mk 1 was replaced by a new version, the Mk iv. Some aircraft were also equipped with a new device known as Terfectos', which emitted a pulse that triggered the IFF (Identification Friend or Foe) sets of German night-fighters and enabled the Mosquitoes to home on to the answering signal.

Nevertheless 100 Group's fighter force never really succeeded in getting to grips with the enemy night-fighters. Quite apart from equipment problems, the Mosquito crews were faced with the formidable task of operating deep inside enemy territory as complete free-lancers, with no help from other quarters. Furthermore enemy fighters had to be intercepted before they entered the bomber stream, because once they were inside it it was extremely difficult to make radar contact with them owing to the profusion of other echoes. The tactics employed by the Mosquitoes usually began with a bombing and cannon attack on enemy night-fighter airfields a few minutes before the bomber stream entered the area of German radar coverage. Other Mosquitoes would work on the flanks of the stream, about forty miles from it and at a higher altitude, in the hope of intercepting enemy fighters before they reached the bombers.

As the bombers were on their way home from the target, more Mosquito fighter-bombers loitered over the German airfields, waiting to catch the night-fighters as they came in to land.

One of the biggest efforts carried out by 100 Group took place on the night of 20/21 March 1945, when the Group mounted a large-scale countermeasures operation in support of a raid by 235 Lancasters and Mosquitoes on the synthetic oil plant at Bohlen, south of Leipzig, which was made in conjunction with a second attack by 166 Lancasters on an oil refinery at Hemmingstedt. The evening's activity began with a 'feint' attack on Berlin by 35 Mosquitoes of the Pathfinder Force at 21.14 hours; a further 27 aircraft raided Bremen a few minutes later. At 01.00 the Bohlen force of Lancasters and Mosquitoes crossed the enemy coast, while 64 more Lancasters made landfall further to the south. The latter aircraft were drawn from Operational Conversion Units, and their task was to carry out a diversionary sweep. At 01.30 41 Lancasters of the Bohlen force broke away and set course northeastwards, just as the first wave of 100 Group Mosquitoes was arriving over the enemy fighter airfields.

At 02.05 14 Halifaxes of 199 Squadron, positioned in a line over northern France, switched on their Mandrel equipment to screen the main bomber force. Fifty minutes later, as the diversionary force of OCU Lancasters turned for home having reached a point just west of Strasbourg, the main bomber stream broke through the Mandrel screen and crossed the Rhine a few minutes later, altering course and heading for Kassel. Further north the 41 Lancasters which had broken away earlier headed for Cologne. Both streams were escorted on their flanks by Mosquitoes, waiting to intercept enemy night-fighters.

The presence of two large bomber formations over German territory — one heading for Kassel and the other apparently positioning to turn towards it at any moment — presented the German fighter controllers with a problem. They could not be certain that the apparent movement towards Kassel was not a feint. On the other hand if they delayed much longer before scrambling the night-fighters, the latter would not have a chance to intercept before the attack took place, should Kassel prove to be the genuine objective. The decision was therefore taken to get the night-fighters — about 120 in all-off the ground and assemble them over Kassel.

As the fighters were taking off, reports began to come in of target indicators going down over Kassel and it seemed as though the controllers' decision had been correct. They had no way of knowing that the TIS were being dropped by a small diversionary force of twelve Mosquitoes, which also discharged bundles of Window, and it was not until several minutes later that the controllers realized that the main force had altered course eastwards, apparently towards Leipzig. They now made frantic attempts to inform the night-fighters of the change of target, but by this time all twenty fighter control channels were being solidly jammed by 100 Group, and there were lengthy delays before the necessary instructions were received by the German radio operators.

At 03.20 the southerly bomber stream split in half, and shortly afterwards target indicators were down on Halle. The bewildered night-fighter crews received yet another series of instructions, and once again found themselves chasing a raid that did not exist. The 'large force' of bombers reported over Halle in fact consisted of twelve Lancasters, dropping Window.

Twenty minutes later, to add to the general confusion, reports also came in of more target markers descending on Bohlen. This time, however, the attack was real. The northern and southern bomber streams joined forces and the first bombs went down on the oil refinery at 03.41. Ten minutes later the last wave of bombers turned for home, leaving the target burning and in ruins. It was at that moment that the first enemy night-fighters arrived in the area. Several were engaged by the 100 Group Mosquitoes patrolling the flanks, but the remainder broke through in time to catch the stragglers among the bombers and shot seven of them down.

As the bomber force droned homewards from Bohlen, the 100 Group Halifaxes which had been orbiting over northern France switched off their Mandrel equipment and carried out a spoof raid towards Frankfurt, dropping Window, in support of the night's second major operation: the attack by 166 Lancasters on Hemmingstedt. This raid took the German defences completely by surprise, and only a handful of night-fighters managed to intercept the attacking force. One Lancaster was shot down over the target, which was eighty per cent destroyed or damaged. Neither the Hemmingstedt plant nor that at Bohlen was able to produce any further oil before the end of the hostilities.

Of the 678 aircraft engaged in these operations two of them — from 100 Grop — failed to return. This worked out at a loss rate of 1.9 per cent — roughly the average for Bomber Command operations during the last weeks of the war. That this low figure was due in no small way to the efforts of 100 Group was not in doubt. Night after night the Group's operations reduced the science of German fighter control to mere guesswork, causing a severe drop in morale among both controllers and night-fighter crews. It must also be remembered that at this stage in the war the German night-fighter *Gruppen* — in common with every other first-line *Luftwaffe* unit — were desperately short of fuel, and consequently every hour spent in chasing a fake raid was a victory in itself. This shortage of fuel restricted the *Luftwaffe* night-fighter sorties to about 80 per night, although 200 aircraft were available on paper, and prevented the fighter controllers from allocating numbers of fighters to patrol different sectors of the sky. Nevertheless the night-fighters that did succeed in getting airborne in the early months of 1945 were almost invariably manned by highly experienced crews, some of them with fifty or more RAF bombers to their credit, and they would have certainly continued to inflict heavy losses on Bomber Command had it not been for the continual radio jamming.

At the end of the war the strength of 100 Group stood at 235 Halifaxes, Mosquitoes, Fortresses and Liberators. In eighteen months of operations the Group's long range fighter force destroyed 236 enemy aircraft in combat, together with 21 more destroyed on the ground. An additional 12 aircraft were claimed as probably destroyed. Sixty-seven of the Group's aircraft failed to return.

7 - Prelude to Overlord

In November 1943 a large number of RAF squadrons were transferred from the various Commands to the 2nd Tactical Air Force, which had been created to provide the necessary air striking power in support of the coming Allied invasion of Europe. It consisted of four Groups: Nos 83 and 84 Groups were to provide tactical support for the 1st Canadian and 2nd British Armies, No. 85 Group was to defend the Allied bridgehead across the Channel once it had been established, and the medium bombers — Marauders, Mitchells, Mosquitoes and Bostons — of No. 2 Group were to strike at communications and supplies behind the enemy lines. There was also a Reconnaissance Wing and an Air Spotting Pool, and the massive task of furnishing air transport and supply fell to No. 38 Group. All these units, together with the mighty power of the United States 9th Air Force, formed the framework of the Allied Expeditionary Air Force, commanded by Air Chief Marshal Sir Trafford Leigh-Mallory. Its total strength was 5,677 aircraft, of which 3,011 were fighters, medium bombers, light bombers and fighter-bombers.

The importance of air power, and particularly of strategic bombing, relative to the success or failure of the invasion, was a subject of constant discussion among the Chiefs of Staff during 1943. In June of that year it seemed that the Anglo-American bombing offensive, launched under the authority of the Casablanca Directive, had fallen far short of its primary goal of destroying the enemy's economy and undermining the morale of the German people. In some fields German war production was actually on the increase; this was particularly true of fighter production, a fact that was giving the Allied leaders cause for concern. The Chief of Staff to the Supreme Allied Commander, Lieutenant-General Frederick Morgan, stated:

The most significant feature of the German Air Force in Western Europe is the steady increase in its fighter strength which, unless checked and reduced, may reach such formidable proportions as to render an amphibious assault out of the question. Above all, therefore, an overall reduction in the strength of the German fighter force between now and the time for surface assault is essential. This condition, above all others, will dictate whether amphibious assault can or cannot be successfully launched on any given date.

This viewpoint with its somewhat pessimistic undertone was not shared by the Allied bomber commanders, who firmly believed — despite the inconclusive results achieved so far — that, in the strategic bomber, they controlled the decisive instrument of modern warfare. General Spaatz, commanding the United States Strategic Air Force, remained to be convinced that an invasion was really necessary. He, together with Air Chief Marshal Sir Arthur Harris and General H. H. Arnold, the USAAF representative on the Joint Chiefs of Staff, still thought that strategic bombing alone could bring about the collapse of Germany. In this the architects of the strategic offensive were in agreement; where they continually failed to agree, on the other hand, was on the choice of targets. Spaatz considered that the enemy's oil resources, on which a nation at war depended, should have the first priority. Harris remained a firm advocate of area bombing, with its attendant massive destruction and effect on the enemy's morale. Other bomber leaders thought that the key to success lay in continual attacks on communications, designed to paralyse the enemy's ability to wage successful war. Because of their belief that the strategic bomber alone was capable of winning the war, the commanders of the Allied strategic air forces tended to neglect or overlook the tactical demands of ground forces. In their opinion the diversion of large numbers of heavy bombers from the strategic to the tactical role was a complete waste of effort; the German armies in the field, formidable though they may be, were powerless to prevent the wholesale devastation by strategic bombing of the homeland it was their purpose to defend.

This viewpoint was totally opposed to that held by the Supreme Allied Commander, General Eisenhower, who stressed that the mighty power of the Allied land, sea and air forces should be forged into three prongs of a single weapon, wielded under the direction of one commander to achieve maximum results. Shortly after his appointment, he stated: 'The strategic air arm is almost the only weapon at the disposal of the Supreme Commander for influencing the general course of action, particularly during the assault phase.' In other words Eisenhower demanded full control of the strategic air forces to fulfil the demands of Overlord, and on this point he was inflexible. 'Unless the matter is settled at once,' he wrote in a memo to Washington dated 22 March 1944, 'I will request relief from this command.' It was not a matter of obstinacy. When Eisenhower wrote that memo, less than ninety days remained before the tentative date of Overlord, and the Supreme Commander wanted the decision to place the strategic air forces in his hands to be taken now, while there was still time to execute a comprehensive plan for their employment in the preliminary 'softening up' and assault phases of the invasion.

Eisenhower was to have his way. But in February and March 1944, while this command struggle went on at top level, another — and often bitter — battle flared up between the air commanders themselves over how best to employ air power in support of the invasion. The principal antagonists were General Spaatz, who remained a strong advocate of hitting the enemy's oil resources at every opportunity, and Air Chief Marshal Sir Arthur Tedder, the Deputy Supreme Commander, who believed that a sustained attack on the German transport system would produce the best results. Broadly, Tedder wanted such an offensive to embrace the disruption of enemy communications by the destruction of railways, rolling stock, marshalling yards, repair and maintenance facilities, roads and bridges — in short, anything that would impede the transfer of German reinforcements to the battlefield.

Tedder's 'Transportation Plan' had, in fact, first been submitted by the Allied Expeditionary Air Force HQ in January 1944. It envisaged an all-out assault lasting ninety days against 72 rail and road targets, 39 in Germany and the rest in France and Belgium. Eisenhower himself thought that the plan would form 'the greatest contribution he could imagine' to the success of Overlord, and Tedder consequently found himself firmly championed. Although the attacks on enemy communications began in February, however, the plan was never implemented on anything like the scale that might have been achieved had it received the full support of the 'Bomber Barons' such as Spaatz and Harris, both of whom felt that it would be a major blunder to divert a large slice of the strategic bombing effort away from attacks on the German industries at a time when the repeated hammer-blows were apparently beginning to have a telling effect. Moreover they pointed out that rail junctions and marshalling yards were among the most difficult of all targets to hit, and that it would be almost impossible to achieve enough destruction before D-Day to prevent the Germans from moving up their reserves as planned.

An assessment of the initial phase of the transport attacks, in March and April 1944, by Air Intelligence, 21st Army Group Headquarters and SHAEF G-2 appeared to bear out these opinions. In fact 21st Army Group scornfully described the attacks as 'pinpricks', hinting that the bombers might have been more profitably employed elsewhere.

What seemed at first sight to be a defeat for Tedder, however — and a victory for Spaatz and Harris — was in reality nothing of the kind. Not for the first time in the history of warfare, the intelligence analysis was wildly inaccurate. It was not until the Allied forces set foot on the Continent in June 1944 and began to push deeper inland, that the full extent of the havoc wrought by the air attacks on enemy communications was appreciated. By D-Day, in fact, the enemy transport system in western Europe was on the verge of collapse — a state of affairs brought about largely by heavy attacks on marshalling yards and repair centres.

The selection of enemy transport targets was the responsibility of a newly formed organization, the Allied Expeditionary Force Bombing Committee. After consultation with transport experts, it was decided to pick locomotive sheds and repair depots as the primary targets, and a list of 80 was drawn up. Of these 37 were allocated to RAF Bomber Command, and the remaining 43 were shared between the 8th US Air Force and Leigh-Mallory's Allied Expeditionary Air Force.

Bomber Command's offensive against the enemy railway system began on the night of 6/7 March 1944, when the marshalling yards at Trappes were attacked by the Lancasters and Halifaxes of Nos 5 and 6 Groups. Between this date and 10 April the Command carried out fourteen operations against eleven rail targets, involving the despatch of 2,513 sorties. Nearly three-quarters of these were flown by the Halifaxes of Nos 4 and 6 Groups. On each raid the target marking was carried out by Oboe-equipped Mosquitoes of the Pathfinder Force, and the results were in some cases far from spectacular. The incidence of gross error on the part of the marker aircraft was far greater than had been anticipated, and this resulted in as many as twenty-five per cent of the main-force bombs falling a considerable distance from the target. The development of new visual marking techniques to assist precision bombing at night consequently became of profound importance, and it was logical that No. 5 Group — many of whose crews had vast experience in carrying out accurate attacks on small objectives — should be allotted the lion's share of this task.

The new precision-bombing tactics that were developed were, in fact, based to a great extent on the operational experience of No. 617 Squadron, which — under the leadership of Wing Commander Leonard Cheshire — had brought low-level visual target marking to a fine art. The deficiencies of existing marking techniques had become only too apparent to Cheshire in the course of three attempts to destroy the Antheor Viaduct in southern France. On each occasion heavy defences had compelled the marker aircraft to release their TIS from not less than 7,000 feet, with the result that all the markers had fallen wide and the viaduct had escaped destruction.

An attack on the Gnome-Rhone aero-engine factory by twelve Lancasters of 617 Squadron on the night of 8 February 1944, however, had produced a far more satisfactory result. This time Cheshire had been able to approach the target at very low level, dropping a cluster of 30-lb incendiary bombs right on the aiming point from a height of only 200 feet. This enabled the remaining crews, bombing from heights of between 8,000 and 10,000 feet, to place their 1,000 and 12,000 lb bombs with remarkable accuracy. The target was totally destroyed, and the surrounding residential areas of Limoges suffered no damage whatsoever. This mission proved that great precision could be achieved with the new stabilized automatic bomb-sight from heights greater than 10,000 feet. It also underlined the importance, in the case of small precision targets, of placing the markers right on top of the aiming point, and there was no escaping the fact that in the Limoges attack this had been possible only because the target had been undefended.

Although the Lancaster was the finest bomber in the world from the point of view of load-carrying capacity, it was highly vulnerable at low level and consequently a far from ideal vehicle for target marking. What was needed was a faster, more manoeuvrable aircraft, one that was a good deal smaller than a Lancaster, but which could nevertheless carry a substantial load of markers and incendiaries deep into enemy territory. The obvious choice was the versatile Mosquito, and on 27 March Cheshire flew to Colby Grange to be checked out on one of these aircraft. He flew his first low-level marking mission in a Mosquito on the night of 5/6 April.

Towards the middle of the month what was in effect No. 5 Group's own Pathfinder Force was formed at Coningsby, in Lincolnshire, with No. 617 Squadron as its nucleus. Three more squadrons — Nos 83 and 97 with Lancasters and No. 627 with Mosquitoes — were transferred to the new formation from No. P48 Pathfinder Group, and the lineup was completed by No. 106 Squadron. On 20 April No. 54 Base, as the formation was designated, undertook its first operation as a complete entity when it was briefed to mark the marshalling yards at La Chapelle, north of Paris, for a force of 5 Group Lancasters.

There were to be two attacks, aimed at separate points in the yards and with an interval of one hour between them. Aircraft of the Pathfinder Force were to mark the target initially, bombing with the aid of Oboe; the aiming points were then to be marked by Nos 83, 97, 617 and 627 Squadrons. In all, 269 bombers were scheduled to take part.

The mission began at 00.03 hours on 21 April, when six Mosquitoes of 627 Squadron arrived over the target area and began discharging Window. The Pathfinder Force aircraft released their green TIS on schedule. These were to have been followed one minute later by a wave of flare-carrying aircraft, but since the TIS failed to cascade immediately, the first wave of flare-droppers orbited the area until a second wave arrived. The latter were equipped with Oboe and consequently were able to drop their flares on target, whereupon the first wave also released their flares. At almost exactly the same moment the original green TIS finally cascaded, forming a brilliant firework display around the marshalling yards. In the intense light Wing Commander Cheshire made a diving run across the target in his Mosquito, locating the aiming point and marking it from low level with red indicators. This process was repeated by a second Mosquito flown by Cheshire's deputy, Flight Lieutenant Fawke. By this time the aiming point was clearly indicated and the main force was instructed to begin its attack.

The second attack an hour later followed a similar pattern. This time the target was marked by Squadron Leader Dave Shannon and Flight Lieutenant Kearns of 617 Squadron, and although the red indicators overshot by about 100 yards they were nevertheless well within the target area, enabling the main force to achieve an excellent bombing concentration.

Subsequent daylight reconnaissance showed that the area around each of the aiming points had been completely devastated, proof enough that the new target-marking techniques worked admirably. The essentials were these: first of all the target was indicated by 'proximity marking' — in other words by markers released blindly with the aid of Oboe; then the flares were dropped, enabling the target to be marked accurately from low level. As a result of the La Chapelle raid it was also recommended that the main force should bomb downwind, as some crews who made their bombing runs into wind reported that the target had been obscured by smoke blowing towards them.

It was clear, however, that the real test of the low-level marking technique would come when it was employed against a target in Germany, and particularly one that was outside the range of Oboe. Because of Bomber Command's heavy commitment to attacks on targets in France during April and May 1944 in preparation for Operation Overlord, Germany's cities and industries had been afforded a breathing space which enabled them to begin a rapid recovery from the year of sustained heavy bombing they had endured between March 1943 and March 1944. Not only were the German war industries fast regaining their normal output capacity, but fighter production was increasing at an alarming rate. So apparent was the lull in heavy attacks on German targets, in fact, that the *Luftwaffe* saw fit to move some of its air-defence units from their bases in the homeland to new locations in France, Holland and Belgium. The immediate result was that Bomber Command's losses during tactical night operations over these areas, which had been negligible during April, began to climb steadily during May, until at the beginning of June they had reached an average of five per cent — a casualty rate that compared with that sustained during the attacks on Germany before the use of Window in July 1943.

It was therefore decided to resume the offensive against the German cities, to slow down the progress of the war industries and also to call a halt to the redeployment of the *Luftwaffe* fighter force, by convincing the Germans that the defence of the Reich was still of the utmost importance. The task of carrying out a major part of this renewed strategic bombing campaign fell to the Lancasters of No. 5 Group, in addition to their considerable effort in the tactical field. So it was that on the night of 22/23 April 1944 No. 5 Group was ordered to mount a maximum effort attack on Brunswick, a target that had grown from the status of a large market town at the beginning of the war to an important centre for light engineering, aircraft components and provisions for the German armies in the field. A force of 265 aircraft was assembled for the raid, and the target marking was to be carried out by No. 54 Base.

Since the weather forecast for the night of the attack was unfavourable, with thick cloud extending east of the Rhine as far as Brunswick and possibly beyond, two Mosquitoes of No. 627 Squadron were to be sent out to a point north of the target half an hour before the main attack was due to begin. These aircraft were to pass a weather report over the VHF to the leader of twenty Lancasters of Nos 83 and 97 Squadrons, which were carrying flares to illuminate the target. If the latter was obscured by cloud the Lancasters were to drop sky markers, providing an aiming point above the cloud layer for the main-force aircraft.

Ten minutes before the main attack four aircraft of the flare force were to drop green target indicators along the approach to Brunswick as a navigational aid for the main force. At the same time ten Mosquitoes were to begin dropping Window between these green indicators and the target itself, a distance represented by about six minutes' flying time. The flare-dropping Lancasters were to arrive over the target in four waves, each wave separated by an interval of one minute. In this way their flares would illuminate the objective for seven minutes, and more flares were to be held in reserve to provide additional illumination during the attack if necessary.

Carefully laid though the plans were, the operation was threatened right from the start by a series of misfortunes. First of all, the 627 Squadron Mosquitoes were unable to transmit their weather reports because of strong VHF interference, which persisted throughout the mission. It later turned out to have been caused by a faulty connection in the VHF set carried by a 627 Squadron Lancaster, which emitted a violent hissing noise. The enemy too made determined efforts to jeopardize the operation by laying dummy TIS, but they made a fundamental mistake: all their dummy indicators were red, whereas the bomber crews had been briefed to look out for only green TIS.

The first cluster of flares to be dropped by the Lancasters went down in the wrong place, about five miles south-west of the objective close to the small town of Wolfenbuttel. These flares were sighted and investigated by Wing Commander Cheshire, who, seeing nothing but open country in their light, waited for more flares to go down in order to identify the target positively. The next batch went down only slightly to the north of the aiming point, on which Flight Lieutenant Fawke of 617 Squadron immediately dropped four red spot fires. Cheshire, flying towards the objective, confirmed that the red TIS were in the right place and ordered four more to be dropped to make certain that the aiming point was clearly marked before the main-force attack began.

Even then the operation failed to go entirely to plan. While the attack was in progress green TIS were dropped to assist in marking the target, as the red spot fires were becoming difficult to see, but these fell well to the west of the town and many crews aimed their bombs at them. Repeated instructions from Cheshire, who was acting as Master Bomber, were not understood because of the persistent interference. Nevertheless severe damage was inflicted on the city, and particularly on the built-up areas to the south of its centre. Only three aircraft failed to return, an amazingly low loss for such a deep-penetration mission into Germany. Only one or two night-fighters were sighted during the attack, and returning crews reported that anti-aircraft defences in the vicinity of the target were light and generally ineffective.

The following night 250 Lancasters of No. 5 Group, with the Pathfinders of No. 54 Base once again leading the way, carried out an even longer penetration into enemy territory against a considerably more dangerous target: Munich, the fourth largest city in Germany and the very centre of Nazi ideology. Apart from its propaganda significance, Munich was a vital railway junction on the main supply route to Italy, and was heavily defended by anti-aircraft guns of every calibre. There were also several night-fighter units in the area, and to lure these away a feint attack was carried out on Milan by six Lancasters of 617 Squadron, which dropped flares and TIS over the Italian city as though in preparation for a major attack.

The main force meanwhile flew south-westwards over France as far as Lake Annecy before turning north-east, dropping slow-burning TIS after several minutes on this new heading to serve as route markers. Two-and-a-half minutes before the first flares were scheduled to go down over the target, eleven Mosquitoes of 627 Squadron arrived in the area and began releasing Window. Four more Mosquitoes, flown by Wing Commander Cheshire, Squadron Leader Shannon and Flight Lieutenants Kearns and Fawke, who were to drop the initial target markers, flew to Munich by a direct route, which involved passing over the formidable defences of Augsburg. Between this point and Munich the aircraft had to fly through a non-stop anti-aircraft barrage. They nevertheless arrived safely over the target just as the first flares were going down.

Cheshire dived down to 700 feet through intense flak, his aircraft lit up by searchlights below and flares dropped by the Lancasters above, and dropped red spot fires on the target at 01.41. Similar work was carried out by the three other Mosquitoes, and throughout the attack aircraft of 617 Squadron kept the objective continuously marked. Despite damage to his Mosquito Cheshire remained over the target for several minutes at a height of 1,000 feet to observe the results of the bombing. On leaving the target, he and the other marker aircraft had to run the gauntlet of a massive searchlight belt that extended for fifty miles west of Munich, and for twelve minutes they were subjected to intense flak.

The damage caused to Munich by the attack was considerable. It was estimated that 663 tons of incendiaries and 490 tons of high explosive had fallen within three miles of the aiming point, creating widespread fires and destroying many of the city's public buildings, as well as large areas of military barracks. Munich's transport system was also badly disrupted for several days. Nine aircraft failed to return from the mission, roughly 3.5 per cent of those despatched.

There was to be no respite for the overworked crews of No. 5 Group. On the night of 26/27 April 226 aircraft were despatched to attack Schweinfurt, the scene of some of the bloodiest encounters of the air war in 1943 between the *Luftwaffe* and the 8th US Air Force. As the Americans knew to their cost, Schweinfurt, the centre of the German ball-bearing industry, was heavily defended by flak. For night defence there was a vast array of searchlights and smokescreens. The five big ball-bearing factories in the town had been severely damaged by the USAAF, but intelligence sources indicated that their production was beginning to pick up rapidly and it was clear that another major attack was necessary.

Once again the bomber force made a lengthy detour across southern France to confuse the enemy defences, but this time the ruse did not succeed and the enemy night-fighters were waiting. The wind also veered and strengthened, delaying the main marker and flare force, which meant that there was a considerable interval between the arrival of the initial markers and the main markers. As a result many of the main-force aircraft had to orbit in the target area, waiting until the aiming point was clearly marked. Despite the difficulties, however, a good bombing concentration was achieved around the aiming point and all five factories were damaged — but the cost to No. 5 Group was high. Twenty-three aircraft failed to return, representing a loss rate of over ten per cent. Among those missing were three marker aircraft of No. 54 Base, together with their highly-trained crews — a loss that 5 Group could ill afford.

Many of the bombers engaged in the Schweinfurt attack were heavily attacked by fighters as they were leaving the target area. One of them, a Lancaster of 106 Squadron, was climbing away when it was 'bounced' by a FW 190 at 20,000 feet. The captain took violent evasive action, but the enemy aircraft scored many hits and a fire broke out near a fuel tank on the upper surface of the starboard wing, between the fuselage and inner engine.

Although wounded by shell splinters, one of the crew members — Sergeant Norman Jackson — volunteered to try and put out the fire. Pushing a hand fire extinguisher into the top of his life-saving jacket and clipping on a parachute pack, Jackson jettisoned the escape hatch above the pilot's head. He then started to climb out of the cockpit and back along the top of the fuselage to the starboard wing. Before he had gone very far, however, his parachute pack accidentally opened and the whole canopy and rigging lines spilled into the cockpit.

Nevertheless Jackson decided to carry on. The pilot, bomb aimer and navigator gathered the parachute together and held on to the rigging lines, paying them out as the airman crawled aft. Eventually he slipped and, falling from the fuselage to the starboard wing, grasped an air intake on the latter's leading edge. He managed to cling on but lost the fire extinguisher, which whirled away in the slipstream. The fire meanwhile was spreading rapidly, and soon searing flames were licking at Jackson's face, hands and clothing. It was not long before the intense pain compelled him to let go; he was swept through the flames and over the trailing edge of the wing, dragging his parachute behind.

When the other crew members last saw Jackson's parachute, its canopy was only partly inflated and it was burning in several places. It seemed as though there was little hope for the flight engineer's survival. By this time the fire was raging uncontrollably across most of the wing, and the pilot ordered the others to abandon the aircraft.

Jackson, however, was still very much alive — although in a pitiable condition. Unable to control his descent because of his severely burned hands, he landed heavily, sustaining a broken ankle. At daybreak, in great pain from his ankle, burns and the wounds he had received earlier, he managed to crawl to a nearby village, where he was taken prisoner. He subsequently made a full recovery in hospital, and on 26 October 1945 he was gazetted for the award of the Victoria Cross.

The battle against the enemy's communications in the west meanwhile continued. Up to the night of 5 June 1944 the Allied Air Forces attacked 80 major road and rail targets on the Continent, dropping 76,200 tons of bombs; 51 targets were destroyed and 25 severely damaged. By 5 June the entire railway system throughout north-west Europe had been seriously dislocated, and railway traffic within 150 miles of the Channel coast had been rendered seventy-five per cent unserviceable. In May 1944 the Tactical Air Forces began a massive assault on railways, roads and rolling stock in the Seine area below Paris, while enemy radar and radio installations were pulverized with rocket attacks and cannon fire. Forty-nine coastal batteries were also attacked, while night intruders and day fighters ravaged the *Luftwaffe* in the air and on the ground.

The *Luftwaffe*, nevertheless, continued to fight back hard, challenging the US 8th Air Force's incursions into German territory with unabated ferocity. It was during this period that the *Luftwaffe* made a brief return to intruder operations, and the success they achieved was out of all proportion to the number of night-fighters involved — which makes it all the more amazing, in retrospect, that the Germans did not devote more of their resources to this task.

On 22 April 1944, for example, twenty-four B-24 Liberators of the 448th Heavy Bombardment Group took off in the late afternoon from Seething, Norfolk, to attack the marshalling yards at Hamm. The bombers were escorted by p-47 Thunderbolt and p-38 Lightning fighters during all but a small part of the round trip, and the attack was carried out successfully against only moderate resistance. As the B-24S crossed the Channel on the homeward leg, however, dusk began to fall and the pilots — unused to night flying — switched on their navigation lights. At that moment, as the formation crossed the coast of Kent, it was attacked by several Messerschmitt 109s. The enemy fighters made two swift passes, damaging several Liberators, then disappeared into the eastern gloom.

The 448th, together with other Groups, carried on towards their Norfolk bases. At 22.00 they sighted the complex of airfields, all brightly lit, and the crews were about to make their run-in and break for landing when they were warned over the R/T to turn immediately towards the coast: Seething and the other bases were under attack by fifteen Ju 88 and Me 410 intruders, which were circling overhead and waiting to shoot down any bomber that attempted to land.

Disaster struck as the Liberators swung out over the coast. Allied anti-aircraft guns suddenly opened up, hitting a B-24 in the lead formation. The stricken bomber dived into the ground near Southwold and exploded. The remainder orbited for a few minutes, then turned back towards Seething. As they flew inland they were attacked by a lone Junkers 88, which shot down a second B-24 near Beccles.

The surviving aircraft of the 448th were by this time desperately short of fuel. Enemy fighters or not, they had to get down somehow. A B-24 began its final approach, sliding in between lanes of tracer put up by the airfield's defences. It seemed as though the bomber was going to make it — and then, to their horror, the crew of a Liberator behind saw a dark shape fasten itself to the leading aircraft's tail. It was a Junkers 88, which opened fire just as the B-24 was touching down. The Liberator began to burn and slewed off the runway; the crew got out safely.

Within minutes Seething aerodrome had been turned into an inferno. In the light of burning aircraft the intruders made one strafing run after another. A Liberator, its hydraulics shot to pieces, belly-landed on the runway and four more bombers ploughed into it.

The intruders attacked five airfields that night: Bungay, Hardwick, Seething, Halesworth and Rackheath. At Rackheath Messerschmitt 410s destroyed two B-24S and a third was shot down by friendly anti-aircraft. Seething's defences also shot down two of their own aircraft. In all, 13

B-24S were destroyed and 2 more were damaged; 38 men were killed and 23 wounded or injured. The Germans lost only one aircraft, a Messerschmitt 410 which was shot down by the gunners of a Liberator near Thurton.

The month between 5 May and 5 June 1944 saw the heaviest period of bombing of the war as the Allied Air Forces maintained a non-stop onslaught on the enemy's communications in France and the Low Countries. As D-Day approached a large proportion of the Allied striking force was earmarked to carry out heavy attacks on enemy coastal batteries and radar installations. Since Allied air supremacy had virtually eliminated *Luftwaffe* reconnaissance flights over the Channel area, the Germans depended almost entirely on their coastal radar to give warning of the approach of an invasion fleet, and the destruction of their radar 'eyes' consequently became of the utmost importance.

By the first week of June 1944 air attack had knocked out some eighty per cent of the enemy's coastal radar capability, and to confuse the remaining radar stations about 250 of the warships that were to accompany the invasion fleet were equipped with radar-jamming transmitters. This in itself, however, was not enough. To ensure complete surprise it would be necessary to mount a decoy operation that would lead the enemy to believe that the main weight of the invasion would fall on a different point of the French coast from that actually intended. As the Allied surface forces would be stretched to their limits in support of the actual invasion it was obviously out of the question to employ a large 'ghost fleet' of vessels to simulate the invasion force. The only real solution was to use aircraft, dropping bundles of 'Window' at precise intervals.

In the early hours of 6 June 1944, as the invasion fleet of over 3,000 Allied vessels turned in towards their objectives on the Normandy coast, eight Lancasters of No. 617 Squadron RAF set out over the Channel towards a point north of Le Havre. The aircraft formed up in two lines, each consisting of four aircraft abreast with 4 miles between each and with a distance of 8 miles between lines. The Lancasters flew a series of thirty orbits, each describing an oblong 8 miles by 2, and each orbit was a mile ahead of the previous one to simulate a surface force moving across the Channel at a speed of about seven knots. On each of the 8-mile legs the Lancasters dropped twelve bundles of 'Window' per minute. To ensure the exceptionally high standard of navigational accuracy required, each aircraft carried two 'Gee' sets. To produce larger echoes on the enemy radar with the passage of time — fostering the illusion that a fleet was heading towards the coast — the size of the 'Window' bundles was gradually increased, and the Lancasters maintained an altitude of 3,000 feet to prevent the bundles from dispersing before they hit the water. As an added precaution, in case the ruse was detected and analysed for what it was by enemy airborne radar, a small force of harbour defence boats and air-sea rescue launches kept station beneath the orbiting Lancasters. The vessels carried a device known as 'Moonshine', which picked up enemy radar pulses, amplified them and retransmitted them, giving a 'solid' radar impression of a large concentration of ships forging slowly ahead. The boats also towed 'Filberts', 29-foot-long barrage balloons with 9-foot-diameter radar reflectors built inside their envelopes. Each Filbert produced an echo similar to that of a 10,000-ton ship.

The Lancasters' mission — code-named Operation Taxable-ended at a point exactly ten miles from Cap d'Antifer, within range of the German coastal batteries. As 617 Squadron returned to base their accompanying boats moored their Filbert floats and laid a smokescreen, at the same time broadcasting recorded sounds of large vessels dropping anchor over powerful loudspeakers. As the boats turned for home a second force of aircraft — this time six Stirlings of No. 218 Squadron, accompanied by six launches — was carrying out Operation Glimmer, a similar mission over the Straits of Dover off Boulogne. Both these missions were so successful that, as the respective forces headed back towards the English coast, the German coastal batteries opened up a furious barrage on a large expanse of empty sea, and when the first Allied troops hit the Normandy beaches the Germans at first believed that the landings were a feint, and that the main assault was about to fall further north. The Panzer divisions that might have destroyed the invasion before it had a real chance of developing were consequently held in reserve to meet a non-existent threat, and when they finally moved towards the Normandy beachheads it was too late and the Allies were firmly ashore.

At dusk on 5 June, almost the whole of RAF Bomber Command stood ready to launch an all-out attack on the German defences along the coast. Knocking out the heavy guns was a formidably difficult task. The sites were very small, they had to be hit during darkness, and the guns were elaborately protected, either by casemates of thick concrete or by solid earthworks. Only a direct hit by a heavy bomb stood any chance of destroying them outright. Nevertheless the bombers did their work well. Before dawn on 6 June they dropped 5,000 tons of bombs on the defences of the 'Atlantic Wall'.

One of the last bombers to leave the target area was a RAAF Lancaster captained by Flight Lieutenant F. L. Merrill, DFC. AS they headed for home the crew saw the first salvoes of heavy shells exploding inland from the guns of the warships accompanying the invasion fleet. A few minutes later the fleet itself came into view, filling the scene as far as the eye could reach as ships of every kind converged in the grey light on the Normandy beaches.

8 - The Day and Night Offensive, June 1944-May 1945

Long before the British, Commonwealth and American forces landed in Normandy, the Allied Air Forces had succeeded in establishing almost total air superiority over the invasion areas. As the troops fought their way towards their primary objectives in the dawn of D-Day, waves of tactical bombers and fighter-bombers continued to batter the German defences ahead of them, while high overhead squadrons of Spitfires, Thunderbolts and Mustangs effectively dealt with the small number of *Luftwaffe* formations that tried to interfere with the landings.

It was only now, as the invasion unfolded, that the effectiveness of the three-month-long Allied bombing offensive against the enemy road and rail network in France was demonstrated. Although the Germans immediately rushed reinforcements to the Normandy area, the chaotic state of the railways prevented them from arriving in time to stop the Allies establishing themselves firmly on the Normandy beaches — and when they did reach the battle zone, they had to try to hold a lengthy front without *Luftwaffe* support and with a totally disorganized communications system to their rear.

Paralysing the enemy's communications remained a top priority task for the strategic air forces, both during the invasion and for a considerable time afterwards. Despite unfavourable weather conditions, with cloud between six tenths and ten tenths hanging low over France for a fortnight after D-Day, Bomber Command and the 8th Air Force carried out a series of heavy raids against the main railway centres: in the Nantes-Angers- Saumur-Tours-Orléans area to cut rail traffic from southern France, in the Paris area to cut traffic from north-eastern and eastern France, and in the Rennes-Pontaubault area to disrupt rail communications from the Brest Peninsula.

One of the most spectacular attacks during this series took place on the night of 8/9 June, when nineteen Lancasters of No. 617 Squadron and four of No. 83 set out to destroy the Saumur tunnel in southern France. This was a vital point on the main line running from the south-west to the Normandy front. The RAF'S task was to seal it and also to knock out a railway bridge at its north-east end. For the first time the Lancasters of No. 617 Squadron carried 12,000-lb 'Tallboy' bombs designed by Barnes Wallis, architect of the mines that had destroyed the Mohne and Eder dams. The Tallboy was a remarkable weapon, having both the explosive power of a high-capacity blast bomb and the penetrating power of an armour-piercing bomb without sacrificing explosive filling for thickness of casing. Its secret lay in its perfect streamlining, which gave it a terminal velocity of 3,600 feet per second — faster than the speed of sound. To achieve maximum penetration it had to be dropped from altitudes of over 8,000 feet, so that a high degree of accuracy was necessary. No. 617's Lancasters were fitted with Mk HA bomb sights, which enabled the highly trained crews to place the 12,000-pounders with an average error of no more than 80 yards from a height of 20,000 feet: a quite acceptable margin, considering the bomb's ability to displace a million cubic feet of earth and form a crater that would take 5,000 tons of soil to fill.

The plan for the attack on the Saumur tunnel called for the four Lancasters of No. 83 Squadron to drop flares over the target, enabling 617's commander — Wing Commander Cheshire — to mark the south-west entrance to the tunnel with red spot fires. The four Lancasters were then to bomb the railway bridge at the north-east end of the tunnel with ordinary 1,000-lb bombs, while the south-west end was to be sealed by 617's Tallboys.

The weather over the target was fair, with the cloud base between 9,000 and 11,000 feet — allowing the Lancasters plenty of height to drop their bombs. Although many of 83 Squadron's flares were dropped wide-the result of poor H2S indications-they provided sufficient light for Cheshire to place his markers within forty yards of the tunnel entrance. Eighteen of 617's Lancasters sighted the markers without difficulty and dropped their bombs from between 8,000 and 10,500 feet after making several dummy runs. The nineteenth crew, unable to locate the markers because of clouds of dust and smoke, dropped their Tallboy on the railway bridge at the other end of the tunnel.

The next day reconnaissance showed that one 12,000-pounder had scored a direct hit on the tunnel entrance, making a crater 100 feet in diameter. Two other bombs had fallen in the cutting leading to the tunnel, effectively blocking it. The tunnel was still unusable two months later, when it was occupied by the American forces that landed in the south of France.

Apart from its offensive against communications, Bomber Command also turned its attention to the concentrations of enemy light naval forces based at Le Havre and Boulogne, as it was feared that they might launch attacks on the Allied convoys ferrying supplies of all kinds to the beachheads. The first of these attacks was made in daylight on 14 June, when a force of Lancasters and Halifaxes bombed Le Havre. In this and subsequent attacks 14 E-boats, 3 R-boats, 3 torpedo boats and 16 other light warships totalling some 15,000 tons were sunk at Le Havre, much of the damage being done by 617 Squadron's 12,000-pound bombs which shattered the concrete E-boat pens. At Boulogne Bomber Command destroyed 7 R-boats, 6 minesweepers and 9 other naval vessels.

The intensive operations in support of the invasion brought the award of the Victoria Cross to yet another member of Bomber Command. It happened on the night of 12/13 June, when No. 419 Squadron RCAF — having recently exchanged its Halifaxes for Lancasters — was engaged in an attack on the marshalling yards at Cambrai. Shortly after midnight Flying Officer G. P. Brophy, the rear gunner of Lancaster A-Able, warned his captain, Flying Officer Art Debreyne, that a Junkers 88 was approaching from behind and below. The Lancaster was just beginning to corkscrew when the port wing and aft section of the fuselage were hit by cannon shells. Fire broke out immediately between the mid-upper and rear turrets. Debreyne ordered the crew to bail out and managed to retain partial control while the forward crew members were leaving via the front hatch. Having remained at the controls for what he considered a long enough period to allow the others to get out, the pilot also jumped at a height of 1,300 feet.

Unknown to the captain, however — the intercom was dead-Brophy was still in the rear turret. As there was no longer hydraulic power to rotate the turret, he had to turn it by hand far enough to permit him to reach his parachute. Having obtained it he began to turn the turret beamwards, intending to bail out directly from his position — but the rotation gear handle came away in his hand and he found himself hopelessly trapped.

Meanwhile the mid-upper gunner, Pilot Officer A. G. Mynarski, had recognized Brophy's plight while on his way to the rear escape hatch. He unhesitatingly made his way through the flames to try to release him, and as he did so his parachute and clothing caught fire. All his efforts to free Brophy were in vain, and in the short time left it was impossible to do more. Brophy realized this and waved Mynarski away, indicating that he should try to save his own life.

Mynarski fought his way back through the flames to the escape hatch. There he paused, turned and — as a last gesture to his trapped friend — stood to attention in his burning flying clothing and saluted before jumping. On the ground Frenchmen watched as he descended like a blazing torch, his parachute and clothing aflame. When they reached him he was beyond all help, and died of severe burns shortly afterwards.

Miraculously the only man who had witnessed Mynarski's courage lived to tell the story. The Lancaster struck the ground in a flat attitude and skidded along for a considerable distance. The vibration freed the rear turret and Brophy was thrown clear. He was knocked out for a while, but regained consciousness to find that he had not suffered serious injury. He succeeded in contacting the French Resistance and returned to England early in September. He at once made the facts of Mynarski's heroism known to the authorities, testifying that his colleague could almost certainly have left the aircraft safely had he not paused to try and effect the rescue. Mynarski must have been fully aware that in trying to free the rear gunner he was sacrificing his own life, but he seemed unaffected by any instinct of self-preservation. On 11 October 1946 Pilot Officer Andrew Charles Mynarski was posthumously awarded the Victoria Cross.

On the night of 15/16 June, while bombing operations in support of the Allied land offensive in Normandy were still in full stride, there came a new and alarming development in the air war: the start of the German V-1 flying bomb attacks on southern England. A large proportion of Bomber Command's strength was immediately diverted to an assault on the V-I launching sites and depots, located in the Pas de Calais. These installations presented difficult targets, being cleverly camouflaged and strongly defended, but thanks to the French Resistance the location of most of them was known to Allied Intelligence. By the end of June Bomber Command had despatched 4,661 sorties against the sites, dropping nearly 16,000 tons of bombs on them for the loss of thirty-eight aircraft. A further 44,335 tons of bombs were dropped in the course of 11,939 more sorties between the end of June and 3 September, when the V-I offensive petered out. Some of the storage depots were located in reinforced underground bunkers or in deep natural caves, and 12,000-lb Tallboy bombs were used against these. One series of caves, running into a limestone hill overlooking the River Oise at St Leu d'Esserent, had been used for years by French mushroom farmers; their roofs were on average twenty-five feet thick. This site was attacked twice by Bomber Command using both conventional 1,000- pounders and Tallboys. Direct hits by the latter, together with massive subsidence caused by near misses, made the entire cave system unusable, while heavy concentrations of 1,000-pounders ploughed up the surrounding area. The railway line leading to the caves — over which the V-Is and their supporting equipment was transported — was completely wrecked, and after the complex was captured by the Allies it took the efforts of five thousand American engineers to get it in working order again.

The same method of attack was used by Bomber Command against several other underground V-1 sites, notably at Siracourt, Watten, Wizernes and Mimoyeques. All these objectives were knocked out by 12,000-lb bombs, while a deluge of smaller 1,000- lb weapons churned up the surrounding area and destroyed access routes.

Vital though it was, Bomber Command's offensive against the v-weapon sites — which amounted to some twenty-five per cent of the Command's total operations during the third quarter of 1944 -represented a serious diversion from the all-important task of supporting the Normandy battle. Nevertheless support operations accounted for thirty-five per cent of the Command's effort during this period, a far from insignificant figure. Much of this work involved direct tactical bombing in daylight of targets on the battlefield, as distinct from attacks on communications behind the battlefront. Large numbers of four-engined bombers were often involved, and their effectiveness was proved during the first attack of this kind, when enemy troop and armoured concentrations were virtually obliterated at Villers Boccage just behind the front line on the last day of June. Several similar assaults were carried out in July-notably on the 18th, when over a thousand aircraft of Bomber Command, together with a force of USAAF bombers, attacked three concentrations of enemy armour and installations in an area between Colombelles, Mondeville, Sanerville, Cagny and Manneville. The object of this attack was to assist the advance of the British 2nd Army, which had become bogged down in the face of strong enemy resistance south of Caen. Since some of the enemy positions were only yards from the Allied lines the bombing had to be highly accurate. It was to the credit of the crews that there was only one serious error, when several sticks of bombs fell on a Canadian battalion and caused many casualties. The attack was generally successful, and the Germans suffered heavy losses in armour. One Panzer company, dispersed and camouflaged in an orchard, was completely wiped out, and other tank units which were less hard hit found it almost impossible to manoeuvre on the badly crated ground. The incessant pounding took its toll of the German infantry too. When the 2nd Army launched its offensive in the wake of the bombardment the British captured many prisoners who were wandering helplessly about, suffering from shock and unable to offer resistance.

The most serious delay caused by the sudden switch to heavy attacks on the v-weapons was to Bomber Command's plans for a large-scale strategic offensive against the enemy's oil resources. The attack on German oil production had already been started by the USAAF, and now, with the invasion well under way, several powerful voices in the Air Staff were raised in favour of Bomber Command's participation in the oil campaign. There was one big question mark, and that was whether the Command — in operations against oil targets in Germany — could maintain the same degree of night precision bombing that had been achieved in support of Operation Overlord.

Despite the doubts it was decided to mount four heavy attacks on the German oil industry in June 1944. The first, on the night of the 12th, was against the Nordstern oil plant at Gelsenkirchen. The main force consisted of 271 Lancasters of Nos 1 and 3 Groups, while target marking was carried out by 17 Mosquitoes and 6 Lancasters of the Pathfinder Force. The marking was accurate (with one exception — a red TI which fell ten miles from the target and was bombed by 35 Lancasters) and 200 crews succeeded in placing their bombs within three miles of the aiming point. Only fifteen direct hits were obtained on the oil plant, but these caused substantial damage to all its vital parts. Seventeen bombers failed to return, of which about 11 were destroyed by night fighters — most of them over Dutch territory as they approached the Zuider Zee on their home run.

Four nights later, on 16 June, 162 Halifaxes of 4 and 6 Groups and 137 Lancasters of 1 and 6 Groups took off to attack the oil plant at Sterkrade. The same tactics were employed, with the target marking carried out by 16 Mosquitoes and 6 Lancasters of the PFF. On this occasion the weather forecast was far from promising, and the actual conditions turned out to be worse than those anticipated, with dense cloud stretching all the way to the target and extending up to 14,000 feet. The bomber stream approached the target in two waves, one entering enemy territory to the north and one to the south of Rotterdam. Despite the cloud which obscured many of the TIS, the bombing was accurate and nine of the Sterkrade installations were damaged. The cost to the attacking force, however, was high. *En route* to the target the bombers passed near the enemy fighter assembly beacon at Bocholt and ran into a strong concentration of night-fighters. The latter took a heavy toll, accounting for 20 of the 31 bombers — mostly Halifaxes — which failed to return that night.

The next oil targets, on the night of 21 June, were at Wesseling and Scholven-Buer. At Wesseling the target was to be marked ill visually by red spot fires dropped by Mosquitoes of No. 5 Group, and if these could not be identified the main force crews were instructed to bomb blindly on their H2s indications. The plant at Scholven was also to be marked visually with red spots, but yellow TIS were also to be dropped by Mosquitoes of the PFF as proximity markers. The Wesseling force consisted of 6 Mosquitoes and 120 Lancasters of 5 Group and 7 Lancasters of 1 Group, while 4 Mosquitoes and 120 Lancasters of 5 Group, 5 Mosquitoes of the PFF and 3 Lancasters of 1 Group were despatched to Scholven.

The result of this twin attack was disappointing: subsequent reconnaissance showed that the only apparent damage had been caused by blast to some oil storage tanks at the north-west corner of the Wesseling plant. The attackers ran into severe and highly accurate radar-directed flak up to 18,000 feet, and higher up-above the cloud layer — the night-fighters were waiting. Thirty-seven Lancasters of the Wesseling force failed to return, as did eight of the Scholven force. Two more aircraft were so badly damaged in combats with enemy fighters that they barely managed to limp back to England.

Only one of the four attacks on oil targets carried out in June 1944, then, had achieved any significant damage, and this fact-together with the heavy losses incurred — dealt a considerable blow to the advocates of precision bombing at night. As far as the losses were concerned, these might well have been equally as high in any kind of night attack over areas strongly defended by night-fighters. More and more the Air Staff's opinion began to swing in favour of large-scale daylight attacks with massive fighter escort -a form of operation that was to be of great significance to Bomber Command in the months ahead. In many quarters, the prospect of using the RAF'S heavy bombers for daylight attacks on a large scale was viewed with serious misgivings, and there was no denying that the small number of daylight attacks on strategic targets carried out by Bomber Command in 1942 had been accompanied by heavy losses. In the summer of 1944, however, the situation was somewhat different. Although the Lancasters could not operate satisfactorily in formation at heights greater than 19,000 feet, where they were extremely vulnerable to flak, they could at least have the benefit of long-range fighter escort — something that had been sadly lacking in 1942-3. With strong fighter escort, the Air Staff felt, there was no reason why the heavy bombers should not penetrate to targets deep inside occupied territory and even in western Germany, provided such targets were not too heavily defended and the attacking forces were carefully routed.

The theory was put to the test in June 1944, when a total of 2,716 daylight sorties were sent out to targets in Occupied Europe. The majority of these were flown by Lancasters and Halifaxes, and the loss rate was only 0.4 per cent — an extremely low casualty figure attributable in the main to the lack of day-fighter opposition. In July the number of sorties despatched was 6,847, and once again the loss rate was only 0.4 per cent. All these sorties, however, had been relatively short-range operations against poorly defended targets, and full fighter cover had been provided by the Spitfires of No. 11 Group.

It was not until the end of August 1944 that RAF heavy bombers penetrated into Germany with fighter escort. On the 27th, 216 Halifaxes of No. 4 Group, together with 27 Mosquitoes and Lancasters of the PFF, were despatched to attack the oil plant at Homburg, in the Ruhr. The bombers were accompanied on the outward trip by nine squadrons of Spitfires from Nos 10, 11 and 12 Groups, which made rendezvous with them near Overflakkee at 17,000 feet. Seven more Spitfire squadrons arrived over the target at the same time as the bombers, providing a strengthened escort on the homeward run. Only one enemy fighter-a Messerschmitt no-was sighted during the entire round trip, and this prudently made no attempt to attack. Despite very heavy anti-aircraft fire over Hamburg all the attacking force returned to base. The target itself was severely damaged.

Bomber Command's next major daylight operation against Germany was carried out in the early evening of 6 September, when 181 Lancasters and Halifaxes from No. 6 Group and the PFF — accompanied by six squadrons of Spitfires and four of Mustangs — were despatched to Emden. The bombing, which began at 18.30, was highly accurate and concentrated around the city centre. Only one aircraft, a PFF Lancaster, failed to return. Five days later, encouraged by these successes, Bomber Command launched three separate attacks in one day against oil targets in the Ruhr. The Nordstern plant at Gelsenkirchen was attacked by 129 Lancasters, Halifaxes and Mosquitoes of 4 Group and the PFF; 116 Lancasters out of 3 and 5 Groups and the PFF were despatched to Kamen; while 134 Halifaxes, Lancasters and Mosquitoes of 6 Group and the PFF hit Castrop Rauxel. Fighter cover for the three assaults was provided by twenty squadrons of Spitfires, three of Tempests and three of Mustangs. No enemy fighters were encountered, and the nine bombers that failed to return were all victims of the flak. All three attacks, particularly those on Kamen and Castrop Rauxel, caused widespread damage.

On 6 October there came a new development in the RAF'S daylight offensive, when Bomber Command authorized the use of the blind bombing system known as G-H, which was first used on the night of 3/4 November 1943 in an attack on the Mannesmann Steel Works near Düsseldorf, and was a highly accurate blind bombing device similar to 'Oboe' but working in the opposite sense. Using G-H, an aircraft transmitted pulse signals to two ground stations, which received them and transmitted them back. The aircraft could therefore continuously measure its distance from two known points and track itself over any target within range of the system, determining its bomb release point with great precision. The range of G-H was about 350 miles at 30,000 feet, much the same as Oboe. Its great advantage, however, was that up to eighty aircraft could operate simultaneously from one pair of ground stations.

The first objective selected for a daylight G-H attack, on 18 October 1944, was Bonn. The force despatched consisted of 128 Lancasters of No. 3 Group, escorted by a large number of Spitfires and Mustangs. Only one enemy fighter was seen, and this was quickly driven off. The bombers approached the target in flights of three, each one led by a G-H aircraft, and the subsequent attack — carried out through broken cloud — caused heavy damage to the centre of Bonn. One Lancaster failed to return.

Meanwhile night attacks on German oil targets continued. In the last two weeks of July Bomber Command struck at Wesseling, Schoven-Buer, Homberg, Bottrop and Wanne-Eickel, and also carried out area attacks on Hamburg, Kiel and Stuttgart. A total of 3,419 sorties were despatched to these targets, and 132 Lancasters and Halifaxes failed to return. Most of the losses were due to enemy night-fighter action. Although the enemy air defences were being thrown into considerable confusion by radio countermeasures, the night-fighters still remained a force to be reckoned with. On the night of 28 July, for example, they accounted for most of the 62 missing bombers out of a force of 803 which attacked Hamburg and Stuttgart.

In August the Command carried out twelve major night attacks on German targets, involving the despatch of 3,764 sorties. The loss was 141 bombers, all of them Lancasters and Halifaxes. During the following month 3,188 sorties were despatched in the course of twelve strategic attacks, but this time the total loss was 69 Lancasters and Halifaxes and three Mosquitoes — a significant drop indicating that the effectiveness of the German night-fighter was on the decline.

In terms of striking power Bomber Command — together with the United States Strategic Air Forces — was now approaching its operational climax. During the last three months of 1944 the Ruhr was subjected to its final and most devastating onslaught, with Bomber Command dropping over 163,000 tons of bombs-four times the weight it had dropped during the same period in 1943. Over half the Command's effort was directed at large industrial cities, the remainder being shared in roughly equal proportions between oil targets, communications and support of the land offensive. In the area bombing offensive sixteen towns were repeatedly attacked, with Duisburg receiving the greatest tonnage of bombs. Duisburg was heavily attacked on four occasions; 13,000 tons of bombs were dropped on it in the course of 3,119 sorties. In one twenty-four-hour period alone 9,000 tons fell on Duisburg. This was on 14 August, the day that saw Bomber Command despatch its largest number of sorties and drop the greatest tonnage of bombs of the entire war. Essen was also attacked four times, receiving 11,500 tons of bombs; Cologne was hit three times with 9,500 tons; one massive attack on Dusseldorf involved the despatch of 992 sorties and the dropping of 4,400 tons of bombs; and a total of 22,000 tons were dropped in the course of other attacks on Bochum, Gelsenkirchen, Dortmund, Hagen, Witten, Oberhausen, Neuss, Solingen, Münster, Hamm, Duisburg and Leverkusen. During this three-month campaign against the Ruhr 136 bombers failed to return, representing a loss rate of less than one per cent. Other area attacks were carried out during the same period on sixteen major towns in northern, southern and south-western Germany. The biggest such attack took place on the night of 19/20 October, when 583 bombers were sent out to drop 2,500 tons of bombs on Stuttgart.

In November 1944 RAF attacks on oil targets, which had been somewhat neglected during October, were once again stepped up. Between the beginning of November and the end of the year Bomber Command carried out twenty-seven heavy attacks on fifteen oil plants, involving the despatch of 5,194 sorties and the dropping of 23,000 tons of bombs. The loss to the Command was 57 bombers. Nineteen of these missions were flown in daylight, and although the flak was usually intense there was little opposition from the enemy night-fighters. Several of the targets were bombed with a high degree of accuracy through complete cloud cover with the aid of G-H.

Bomber Command also made several notable precision attacks on small strategic targets during the last four months of 1944. The first of these was carried out against the Dortmund-Ems Canal on the night of 23/24 September by 99 Lancasters of No. 5 Group. The crews achieved an impressive bombing concentration, and several direct hits were obtained on both branches of the canal. Subsequent reconnaissance showed that an eighteen-mile stretch of the canal had been almost completely drained, with strings of barges stranded in the mud on the bottom. Nevertheless repairs were quickly effected, and by the end of October the canal was fully operational again. On the night of 4/5 November No. 5 Group made a second attack, this time with 170 heavy bombers, and once again serious breaches were torn in the embankments. The eastern branch of the canal — the narrower of the two waterways — was rendered completely irreparable and was sealed off by the Germans, but the western branch was in service again within three weeks. On 21/22 November 128 Lancasters of 5 Group attacked yet again, aiming from 4,000 feet at the aqueduct carrying the western branch of the canal over the River Glane. Four direct hits were achieved on the aqueduct, and a 190-foot breach was torn in the embankment south of the aiming point, releasing large quantities of water into the surrounding countryside.

By the end of December, however, German forced labour gangs — working day and night — had once more repaired most of the damage, and the flow of canal traffic continued. On i January 1945 No. 5 Group sent out a fourth striking force, this time in daylight. Hits were again achieved on the aqueduct, the embankment was breached and the safety gates were wrecked. On this occasion delayed-action bombs were dropped to hinder the work of repair.

During this attack a Lancaster of No. 9 Squadron was hit by a heavy shell in front of the mid-upper turret just after its bombs had been released. Fire broke out and dense smoke filled the fuselage. A moment later the nose of the aircraft was also hit and an inrush of air, clearing the smoke, revealed a scene of utter devastation. Most of the perspex screen of the nose compartment had been shot away, gaping holes had been torn in the canopy above the pilot's head, the intercom wiring was severed and there was a large hole in the floor of the aircraft. Bedding and other equipment were badly damaged or burning, and one engine was on fire.

The wireless operator, Flight Sergeant George Thompson, saw that the gunner was unconscious in the blazing mid-upper turret. Without hesitating, he went down the fuselage into the fire and the exploding ammunition. He pulled the gunner from the turret and, edging his way round the hole in the floor, carried him away from the flames, extinguishing the gunner's burning clothing with his bare hands. In the process he himself sustained serious bums on his hands, face and leg. A few moments later Thompson noticed that the rear gun turret was also on fire. Despite his own severe injuries he made his way painfully to the rear of the fuselage where he found the rear gunner with his clothing alight, overcome by smoke and flames. Braving the inferno for a second time, he extricated the helpless gunner and carried him clear, again using his badly burnt hands to beat out the flames that licked over his colleague's clothing.

Although he was by this time almost exhausted, Thompson fought his way back through the burning fuselage to report to the pilot, clinging to the sides with his burnt hands to negotiate the hole in the floor. As he did so, the flow of cold air caused him intense pain and frostbite developed. His condition, in fact, was so pitiful that the pilot failed to recognize him.

Forty minutes later the pilot crash-landed the Lancaster in friendly territory. For three weeks George Thompson clung doggedly to life before finally succumbing to his terrible bums. One of the gunners also died, but the other survived to testify to the wireless operator's supreme courage — courage which, on 20 February 1945, was recognized by the posthumous award of the Victoria Cross.

The daylight raids on the Dortmund-Ems Canal, and other major daylight attacks mounted by Bomber Command during the last weeks of 1944, tended to be overshadowed by the more spectacular precision attacks carried out during this period by the Lancasters of No. 5 Group, and principally by No. 617 Squadron. On 7 October, for example, thirteen Lancasters of No. 617, led by Wing Commander J. B. Tait, set out to attack the Kembs Dam, which lay on the upper Rhine north of Basle. The Germans intended to release the massive volume of water contained by the dam to block the Allied advance across the upper Rhine, but this plan was effectively forestalled by 617 Squadron. Attacking from as low as 600 feet in the face of intense light flak, the Lancasters' Tallboy bombs breached the structure and released the pent-up waters.

Another daring and spectacular precision attack in which 617 Squadron took part was against the German battleship *Tirpitz*. At the end of August 1944 the mighty warship — having recovered from damage sustained in previous attacks by submarines and naval aircraft — lay at anchor in the Norwegian Kaa Fjord, apparently ready to put to sea once more. The presence of the 45,000-ton warship in northern waters represented a considerable threat to convoys taking supplies to Russia. The largest and most heavily armed of Germany's line of battleships, she would almost certainly be able to wreak fearful havoc on the northern sea routes before the Allies could hunt her down.

No. 5 Group, therefore, was instructed to assess the possibility of destroying her before she left her lair, using 12,000-lb bombs. It was a formidable task. For a start, Kaa Fjord lay a thousand miles from the nearest British airfield. Then there was the weather problem to be considered. The northern coast of Norway was normally covered by low-lying stratus cloud during the latter part of the year, and relatively clear weather could be expected on only three days in any one month. The battleship herself was well protected in the narrow fjord by smoke screens and by antiaircraft guns of every calibre, sited around the fjord and on flak ships. In addition there was the Tirpitz's own armament of 16 heavy and 16 light guns. She was also heavily armoured, particularly around the gun turrets and magazines: her armour plating was in two layers, the upper two inches and the lower more than three inches thick. The Tallboy was the only bomb in existence with a chance of penetrating it.

To solve the range problem agreement was reached with the Russians for the Lancasters of Nos 9 and 617 Squadrons to strike at the *Tirpitz* from the Soviet airfield of Yagodnik, on the Archangel Peninsula. The organizational difficulties entailed by such a move were considerable. Joint plans had to be thrashed out for the accommodation of air and ground crews, the servicing of the bombers, and the standardization of air traffic control procedures, recognition signals and radio frequencies. In addition the RAF contingent needed 60,000 gallons of 100-octane fuel, 500 gallons of oil and 15 of glycol, all of which had to be procured from Soviet sources.

Despite the general confusion, 38 Lancasters of the two squadrons set out for North Russia on the evening of 11 September 1944. Of this force, which ran into appalling weather *en route*, one aircraft aborted and returned to Britain when its Tallboy bomb broke loose and had to be jettisoned, 6 more crash-landed in Russia and had to be abandoned, and 2 were immediately placed unfit for operations on arrival at Yagodnik. Two Liberators carrying the RAF ground crews arrived safely, as did a weather reconnaissance Mosquito and a Lancaster carrying an RAF film unit.

On 15 September 28 Lancasters took off from Yagodnik to attack the battleship, which had now moved to a new location in Alten Fjord for extensive repairs to be carried out. No problem was envisaged with the weather, for the reconnaissance Mosquito had surveyed the bombers' route earlier and had reported that conditions were favourable. The main obstacle to the success of the mission was likely to be the massive defensive smokescreen which the Germans were known to be capable of laying across the *Tirpitz's* anchorage in a very short time.

The plan called for the bombers to attack in two waves. The first, consisting of 21 Lancasters flying in sections of 5 and carrying Tallboys, was to bomb from between 14,000 and 18,000 feet, while behind them at between 10,000 and 12,000 feet came 6 more Lancasters carrying 2,000-pound 'Johnny Walker' anti-shipping bombs. Initially the whole force was to make its approach at 1,000 feet to achieve the maximum element of surprise. This height was to be maintained until the Finnish border was reached, when the bombers were to climb to between 2,000 and 3,000 feet above their bombing height. This would enable them to make the actual bombing run in a shallow dive, affording the extra speed that would be vital if the bombs were to be released before the enemy smoke-screen had time to form.

Apart from a major course alteration made necessary by the Tallboy-carrying Lancasters straying off track, the flight to the target was uneventful. As they approached the fjord under an almost cloudless sky the Lancaster crews had a clear view of the battleship, stark against the shining water. The smokescreen quickly began to form and the *Tirpitz* was soon obscured, but five Tallboys went down in her immediate vicinity during the next sixty seconds. The crews that followed took the battleship's flak bursts as their aiming point, and some felt sure that more than one hit had been obtained. There was, however, no way of obtaining any confirmation at this stage, for as the Lancasters left the target area the whole fjord lay under a dense blanket of smoke. Post-raid reconnaissance was also frustrated by cloud, which began to creep across the sky soon after the attack, and when the reconnaissance Mosquito arrived over Alten Fjord some two hours later its crew got only a brief glimpse of the battleship through a ragged gap.

In fact the *Tirpitz* had been damaged to a far greater extent than any of the attacking crews dreamed. She had sustained a direct hit on the bows, which were almost completely destroyed from the stem to the forward turret, and her main engines were also damaged. It was estimated that even if she could reach a north German shipyard with full repair facilities, it would be at least nine months before she could be made battleworthy again. The Germans, however, declined to risk the battleship in a slow voyage down the Norwegian coast. Instead she steamed out of Alten Fjord at six or seven knots to a new anchorage at Tromso, from where it was planned that her heavy armament would help repel an Allied invasion of northern Norway. She was protected from underwater attack by a double net barrage, and from air attack by smokescreens, anti-aircraft batteries on the shore and two flak ships, *Nymph* and *Thetis*.

The British Admiralty had at this stage no way of knowing that the *Tirpitz's* fighting days were over. As far as naval intelligence was concerned, Tromso might simply be a staging point for some other destination. At any rate the warship was still afloat, and as such she continued to represent a threat to the Allied convoys. By 24 October another plan had been devised for an attack on the battleship in her new anchorage, and Nos 9 and 617 Squadrons were once more working out the details of the operation.

This time, since Tromso was some 200 miles closer to the British Isles than Alten Fjord, it was decided to launch the attack from a home base. The round trip involved a flight of 2,250 miles, so to compensate for the weight of their Tallboys and the extra fuel that would have to be carried the Lancasters were stripped of all equipment, including mid-upper gun turrets, that was not considered absolutely necessary. The front guns and ammunition, most of the oxygen bottles and armour plating were all removed. Since no enemy fighters had been encountered during the previous attack the elimination of most of the Lancasters' firepower seemed a justifiable risk, and as all the flight with the exception of the actual attack was to be carried out at no more than 2,000 feet the oxygen would not be missed. Even with all these weight-saving precautions the bombers' fuel would be marginal, and pilots were told that any Lancaster with less than 900 gallons remaining after the attack was to carry on and land at Yagodnik or Vaenga, in Russia.

On the morning of 29 October the strike force was finally ready. It consisted of eighteen Lancasters of No. 617 and eighteen of No. 9, under the command of Wing Commanders J. B. Tait and J. M. Bazin respectively. The aircraft took off in pouring rain and reached the target area at 09.00. The crews had a clear view of the *Tirpitz* as they began their run-in, but at the very last moment low cloud drifted in from the sea and obscured the anchorage. Thirty-three aircraft attacked through heavy flak and dropped their Tallboys, aiming through partial gaps in the cloud, but they were able to claim only one near miss. One aircraft was damaged by flak and force-landed in Sweden; the remainder returned safely to base.

For twelve days the two squadrons stood by, waiting for a favourable opportunity to strike at the battleship once more. On 11 November the weather reports were promising, and the Lancasters flew to Lossiemouth in Scotland to prepare for the mission. At 02.00 the following morning thirty bombers, each armed with a Tallboy, set course north-eastwards towards the Norwegian coast. At the first sign of dawn the force turned east and flew towards the sunrise, crossing the black crags of the Norwegian coast before turning north again. The thunder of their Merlins reverberated from the mountain slopes as they flew low over the barren landscape, crossing great fields of snow that glowed pink in the sun's rays.

The sky was brilliantly clear, and the crews were able to pick out landmarks so far ahead that they had an unreal sense of hanging motionless. Bals Fjord crept into view, and beyond it a huge mountain that hid the Tirpitz's lair. As the distance decreased, more of Tromso Fjord slid into their field of vision — and suddenly they saw the *Tirpitz*. Even at a distance of twenty miles the black silhouette of the battleship appeared immense, looking for all the world like a great spider nestling in the middle of her web of anti-submarine booms. There was no cloud, no smokescreen; the mighty warship lay naked.

Suddenly the *Tirpitz* opened fire, her armament hurling shells towards the bombers until she was obscured by rolling clouds of smoke. Then the flakships and the batteries on shore joined in, and the Lancasters bucked in the shock-waves of countless shell-bursts. The pilots stuck to their headings, following their bomb-aimers' instructions, and at 09.40 the leading aircraft — flown by Wing Commander Tait — released its bomb.

More bombs went down as Tait dived away to port. They exploded on or around the battleship, raising immense columns of smoke and water. As Tait and his crew watched, a column of steam shot up to a height of 300 feet, penetrating the darker clouds of smoke that shrouded the *Tirpitz*.

Following the main force came a Lancaster of No. 463 Squadron, filming the attack. As it ran overhead, its crew saw the great warship slowly capsize, torn apart by two direct hits. When a Mosquito photographed the scene two hours later, the *Tirpitz* had completely turned turtle in the shallow waters of the fjord, her superstructure resting on the bottom. So it was that Bomber Command, at a cost of one aircraft which crash-landed in Sweden, destroyed the pride of Hitler's navy and shattered what remained of Germany's challenge on the high seas.

The Mosquitoes of No. 2 Group too maintained their tradition of skilful precision attacks in the closing months of the war. They had begun the year well. In February 1944 2 Group Mosquitoes led by Group Captain Percy Pickard — who lost his life in the raid — blasted a hole in the wall of Amiens prison, enabling more than two hundred French political prisoners and resistance workers to escape, and two months later Mosquitoes of No. 613 Squadron destroyed the Gestapo headquarters at The Hague in what an Air Ministry bulletin later described as 'probably the most brilliant feat of low-level precision bombing of the war'.

On October 31 1944 No. 2 Group struck at a similar target: the Gestapo headquarters at Aarhus in Denmark. Led by Wing Commander R. W. Reynolds, twenty-five Mosquitoes drawn from Nos. 21, 464 and 487 Squadrons took part in the attack. Since the HQ was located in two adjoining buildings which had previously formed part of the University of Aarhus, the Mosquitoes had to go in at extremely low level in order to pinpoint the target accurately and avoid the possibility of damaging other Danish property. The twenty-five aircraft took off from Thorney Island at 07.00 and set course across the North Sea, escorted by eight Mustangs. The Mosquitoes carried a total of thirty-five 500-lb bombs fitted with eleven-second delayed action fuses.

The target area was reached without incident, the Mustang escort beating up enemy trains and other targets of opportunity as they raced across the Danish landscape at low level. The Mosquitoes swept across the Gestapo HO like a whirlwind and unloaded their bombs into the centre of it, leaving it shattered and ablaze. One Mosquito actually hit the roof of the building, losing its tailwheel and half its port tailplane. It nevertheless managed to reach England safely together with all the others. More than two hundred Gestapo officials were killed in the attack, and all the files on the Danish resistance movement were destroyed in the subsequent fire.

On 31 December Mosquitoes of No. 627 Squadron carried out an equally successful attack on the Gestapo headquarters in Oslo, and on 21 March 1945 Mosquitoes of Nos 21, 464 and 487 Squadrons made a daring low-level attack on the main building of the Gestapo HQ in Copenhagen. Although the target was completely destroyed, the success of this mission was marred by the fact that one of the Mosquitoes, hit by flak, crashed on a convent school and killed eighty-seven children.

In December 1944 much of the Allied strategic bombing effort was diverted to tactical operations in support of the land offensive in Belgium, temporarily reeling under the impact of the last German offensive on the Western Front: Field-Marshal von Rundstedt's armoured counter-attack in the Ardennes. Supported by the remnants of the *Luftwaffe*, which launched a highly effective surprise attack on Allied air bases in Belgium and Holland on New Year's Day 1945, the German push met with some initial success. Bomber Command and the US 8th Air Force carried out intensive daylight attacks on enemy armour and troop concentrations and against railheads, and by the middle of January 1945 the Germans' last gamble had ended in failure. The swift German collapse was due to three main factors: a critical shortage of tanks and aircraft to support such a large-scale operation, a shortage of fuel and oil reserves, and the disrupted condition of the German transport system. All three were the direct result of Allied strategic bombing over the preceding months.

The end for Germany came quickly now. The Allied Air Forces roved virtually unopposed by daylight over the length and breadth of the shattered Reich, striking at a steadily decreasing list of strategic and tactical targets. Between 1 January and 8 May 1945 RAF Bomber Command — with a daily average of 1,500 bombers available for operations — dropped more than 181,000 tons of bombs, one-fifth of the Command's total for the entire war. During this period the Command launched 67,483 sorties for the loss of 608 aircraft, devoting the main part of its effort to oil targets and industrial cities. Thirty of the latter were attacked in January, February and March, twelve of them in daylight. The smallest of these raids was carried out on the night of 22 January, when 152 bombers were despatched to Gelsenkirchen, and the largest was made in daylight on 12 March when 1,079 Lancasters, Halifaxes and Mosquitoes dropped 4,851 tons of bombs on Dortmund. The total number of bombers sent out against Dortmund on this occasion was actually 1,107, the largest number ever despatched by Bomber Command in one raid against a single target.

In terms of destruction achieved the most effective of all these area attacks was that carried out against Dresden on the night of 13/14 February, when 805 bombers struck at the town in two waves. The pretext for the assault on Dresden, in which large areas of the city were razed to the ground by firestorms and in which at least 80,000 people died, was that it was a key base and communications centre for the German armies facing the advancing Russians in the east. Although the attack was made primarily at the request of the Soviet Government, controversy still rages over the justification for it. Be that as it may, the fact remains that Dresden is to this day the symbol of the terrible power of conventional strategic air warfare.

The area attacks on Germany's cities by Bomber Command involved the despatch of 15,588 sorties for the loss of 240 aircraft. Ten per cent of this loss was sustained on the night of 16/17 March, when 277 Lancasters and 16 Mosquitoes were despatched to Nuremberg. The enemy night-fighter force was unexpectedly active and 24 aircraft failed to return.

None of the RAF'S heavy-bomber raids were directed against Berlin in 1945. However, beginning on the night of 20/21 February, the Mosquitoes of No. 2 Group began a series of thirty-six consecutive attacks on the German capital. In 3,900 sorties the Mosquitoes dropped over 4,400 tons of bombs, including 1,800 four-thousand-pounders. Fourteen of them failed to return.

Bomber Command also carried out a sustained offensive against the enemy's oil targets between January and April 1945, making 74 raids on 49 objects. Of these missions 38 were flown a night and 36 in daylight, many of the latter delivered through ten-tenths cloud with the aid of G-H. One of the most destructive attacks was carried out against Scholven-Buer in daylight on 10 March, when 153 Lancasters dropped 755 tons of bombs on the target through the overcast. The plant was completely devastated and all the bombers returned to base.

Precision attacks also continued. In February 1945 No. 617 Squadron received the first examples of a new and formidable weapon designed by Dr Barnes Wallis, a ten-ton bomb known as 'Grand Slam'. This 22,000-lb monster was first used operationally on 14 March 1945, when one was dropped on the Bielefeld Viaduct by a 617 Squadron Lancaster piloted by Squadron Leader C. C. Calder. The objective was completely destroyed. Forty more Grand Slams were dropped before the end of hostilities, some of them against naval targets such as the u-boat pens at Farge, attacked by Nos 9 and 617 Squadrons with Tallboys and Grand Slams on 27 March. Tallboys were again used against the Kriegsmarine on 9 April, when Bomber Command capsized the German pocket battleship *Admiral Scheer* during an attack on Kiel. The Germans had planned to use the heavy armament of the *Scheer* — which had been the objective of the very first raid carried out by Bomber Command during the Second World War, on 4 September 1939-in a defensive role against the Allied advance. Two more warships, the cruisers *Admiral Hipper* and *Emden*, were so severely damaged in the same attack that they were unfit for further use.

Relentlessly the onslaught continued. On 25 April 318 Lancasters of Nos 1, 5 and 8 Groups attacked Hitler's mountain retreat and the adjacent ss barracks at Berchtesgaden. This raid was carried out at the request of the United States 7th Army, whose only opposition in southern Germany came from fanatical ss elements. Later, when the American troops advanced on Berchtesgaden, they reported that the entire mountainside was still 'smoking and smouldering' from the effects of the bombardment. That afternoon 468 Halifaxes, Lancasters and Mosquitoes of Nos 4, 6, 8 and 100 Groups struck hard at enemy coastal gun batteries on the island of Wangerooge.

After nightfall ninety-two Lancasters attacked an oil refinery and storage tanks at Vallo, near Tonsberg. It was the last time that the main-force heavy bombers of the RAF raided the enemy in the Second World War.

Meanwhile the Fortresses and Liberators of the USAAF spun their contrails daily across the skies of ruined Germany, their long-range escorts of Mustangs and Thunderbolts swarming over the dwindling squadrons of the *Luftwaffe* and turning the enemy's fighter airfields into graveyards of shattered aircraft. Nevertheless the *Luftwaffe* was still in evidence. Despite the strategic air offensive against Germany's aircraft factories and workshops, the Germans succeeded in maintaining a monthly production of between 1,200 and 1,500 military aircraft-a figure that rose to 2,325 in November 1944. Even these totals, however, were not enough to compensate for the staggering combat losses suffered by the *Luftwaffe* in 1944-5. In July 1944, for example, 2,627 single-engined fighters were delivered to the *Luftwaffe's* first-line units — but in the same period over 3,000 machines were destroyed in combat and accidents.

The only apparent answer to this appalling rate of attrition was to mass-produce a fighter superior to any in service with the Allies, which would regain control of the German sky and deal crippling punishment to the Allied strategic bombers. Such an aircraft-the twin-jet Messerschmitt 262-was already in existence, but its entry into service had been subjected to serious delays — not the least of which was Hitler's insistence that it should be converted for use as a 'reprisal bomber', a role to which it was totally unsuited. By November 1944, however, the 262 was being mass-produced in its original role of *Kampfzerstdrer* — bomber-destroyer — and in January 1945 at least two hundred were in first-line service.

One of the first encounters between the Allies and the Me 262 occurred on 25 July 1944, when a Mosquito of No. 544 Squadron took off from RAF Benson to carry out a photoreconnaissance mission over Munich. The aircraft was at 29,000 feet not far from its objective when the pilot, Flight Lieutenant A. E. Wall, sighted a twin-engined aircraft closing very rapidly 400 yards astern. Wall at once applied full power but the enemy aircraft rapidly overtook the Mosquito and opened fire. Wall took violent evasive action and shook off the fighter three times, but each time it closed in again, cannon blazing. Several of its shells struck home before Wall reached cloud cover. When he emerged into clear skies a few minutes later, there was no sign of the Me 262. The Mosquito went on to make an emergency landing in enemy territory — the first aircraft to be damaged in combat with a jet.

On 28 July it was the Americans' turn to confront the *Luftwaffe's* new weapon. Nine p-51 Mustangs were escorting a wing of B-17S at 25,000 feet over Merseburg when the pilots spotted two contrails at six o'clock, five miles away and several thousand feet higher up. The Mustang leader's report describes the action:

I identified them immediately as the new jet propelled aircraft. Their contrails could not be mistaken and looked very dense and white, somewhat like an elongated cumulus cloud some threequarters of a mile in length. My section turned 180 degrees back towards the enemy, which included two with jets turned on and three in a glide without jets operating at the moment. The two I had spotted made a diving turn to the left in close formation and feinted towards the bombers at six o'clock, cutting off their jets as they turned.

Our flight turned for a head-on pass to get between them and the rear of the bomber formation. While still 3,000 yards from the bombers, they turned into us and left the bombers alone. In this turn they banked about 80 degrees but their course changed only about 20 degrees. Their turn radius was very large but their rate of roll appeared excellent. Their speed I estimated was 500 to 600 miles per hour. Both planes passed under us 1,000 feet below while still in a close formation glide. In an attempt to follow them, I Split-S'd. One continued down in a 45-degree dive, the other climbed up into the sun very steeply and I lost him. Then I looked back at the one in the dive and saw he was five miles away at 10,000 feet.

On this occasion the brush had been with rocket-propelled Messerschmitt 163s, a type that was encountered again the following day by P-38 Lightnings escorting a damaged B-17 at 11,000 feet over Wesermunde. A Me 163 made a single power-off pass at the bomber then went into a climb. Both P-38s followed it and managed to score some hits before the rocket fighter rolled over and dived into the overcast below. A few days later, however, the enemy fighters gained the upper hand when three Me 163s swept through a formation of Mustangs escorting B-17S over Magdeburg. Before the startled American fighter pilots had time to react, three Mustangs were going down in flames. The 163s escaped easily.

It was in March 1945 that the Allies felt the full impact of the enemy jet fighters. On the 18th 1,250 American bombers set course for Berlin to deliver the heaviest attack of the whole war on the German capital. A few miles short of the target the formations were attacked by 37 Me 262s of *Jagdeschwader* 7, which shot down 19 bombers for the loss of 2 of their own number. Most of the bombers were destroyed by R4M air-to-air rockets, 24 of which were carried by each Me 262 on underwing rails. On 4 April the jets repeated their success when 49 Me 262s of JG 7 attacked 150 B-17S over Nordhausen and destroyed 15 of them. Four days later JG 7 — this time directing its attack against the escorting American fighters — demonstrated the Me 2625s enormous speed advantage over piston-engined fighters by shooting down 28 Mustangs, Lightnings and Thunderbolts in air battles that raged across northern and central Germany. Nevertheless there was no escaping the fact that on this same day no fewer than 133 piston-engined Messerschmitt 109s and Focke-Wulf 190s were destroyed by Allied fighters. No matter how many successes were registered by the German jets, they were too few and it was too late; the Allies remained firmly in control of the air.

The RAF too had several encounters with German jet and rocket fighters. On 8 February 1945, for example, a Me 262 was shot down by two gunners in a Halifax of No. 427 Squadron engaged in a daylight raid on Goch, while the gunners of another Halifax of the same squadron claimed a Me 163 as probably destroyed.

For the RAF the most serious conflict with the jets came on the night of 30/31 March and the next day. One German night-fighter squadron, 10/NJGII, was equipped with Me 262s, and on 30/31 March Oberleutnant Walter — the commander of this unit — shot down no fewer than 4 Mosquitoes on the approaches to Berlin. The following morning, Halifaxes of No. 6 Group- operating over Hamburg without fighter cover because they arrived over the target ten minutes late — were bounced by 30 Me 262s, and 8 Halifaxes were shot down.

Another revolutionary type in *Luftwaffe* service during the closing months of the war was the Arado 234 twin-jet reconnaissance bomber. This aircraft became operational with the *Luftwaffe's* 1. Staffel/Versuchsverband — based at Juvincourt, near Rheims — in July 1944, and made a series of successful highspeed reconnaissance sorties over the Allied beachheads in Normandy. In August the unit pulled back to Volkel in Holland and in September it was based at Rheine, in Germany, from where it carried out a number of high-level sorties over the east coast of Britain — the only enemy jet squadron to do so. Early in 1945 one Ar 234 reconnaissance squadron was based in Denmark and two more in Germany; a fourth, *Sonderkommando* Sommer, was sent to Trieste in March 1945 to support the German Army in northern Italy. Equipped with three Ar 234s, it flew many unmolested sorties over the Leghorn and Ancona sectors of the front.

A bomber variant, the Ar 234B, entered service with KG 76 at Lonnewitz in October 1944, and operated in support of the German offensive in the Ardennes a few weeks later, KG 76's most intensive period of operations was in March 1945, when one of the unit's most vital missions was the attempted destruction of the famous bridge at Remagen, captured by us armoured spearheads.

It was futile; Germany was plunging towards catastrophic defeat. On 30 April Hitler committed suicide, with Russian shells exploding round the *Fuhrerbunker* in Berlin. The country's greatest cities were devastated wildernesses; its industries were in ruins; its communications system tom asunder by the weight of Allied air attack. The *Luftwaffe's* latest jets stood idle on their bomb-cratered airfields and among the trees along the sides of stretches of autobahn hastily converted into runways, crippled by the swarming Allied fighters and lack of fuel. The piston-engined Focke-Wulfs and Messerschmitts, flown for the most part by hopelessly inexperienced pilots, were massacred day after day.

On 10 April 1945 an Arado 234 jet of 1 (*Fernaufklarungs-gruppe*) 33 took off from Stavanger-Sola in Norway. It headed out over the North Sea and made landfall over the Orkneys, its contrail describing a wide arc over the naval base at Scapa Flow. The Arado flew south for a time across Scotland, reaching the Firth of Tay before setting course for Norway once more. It was not intercepted.

Five and a half years earlier a Dornier 17 of 1 (F) 33 had photographed units of the British Fleet in Scapa Flow only a matter of hours after the outbreak of war. To this same unit now fell the honour — albeit a bitter one — of carrying out the *Luftwaffe's* last sortie over the British Isles. And there was something more: the opening of a new era in the history of air warfare, etched in chalk across the sky behind the Arado's jet engines.

Germany was defeated, but for the Allied Air Forces there remained two tasks to be carried out. On 26 April the British and Americans began an airlift of ex-pows from Germany to the UK. This task, code-named

Operation Exodus, lasted until 1 June, during which time aircraft of Bomber Command alone flew more than 75,000 prisoners home.

On 29 April the RAF and USAAF initiated Operation Manna — the dropping of food and medical supplies to the Dutch population. Dropping zones were marked by aircraft of the Pathfinder Force, and up to 8 May-the date of Germany's unconditional surrender — the RAF delivered 10,000 tons of provisions to Holland by air.

So, on a note of humanity and mercy, the greatest fighting machine in history ended the conflict in Europe.

9 - The Strategic Air Offensive against Japan, 1944-5

In the Pacific theatre strategic bombing did not enter into the picture until the summer of 1944. The Japanese never had a long-range bomber force at any stage in the war, their offensive air power being dictated entirely by the tactical requirements of the Army and Navy, and the whirlwind occupation of the Pacific chain of islands by Imperial Japanese forces after the American defeat at Pearl Harbour effectively placed Japan itself out of range of the USAAF'S B-17S and B-24S.

The course of the Pacific war was dominated throughout by the use of naval air power on an unprecedented scale, with powerful American carrier task forces progressively destroying the might of the Imperial Japanese Navy and striking hard at the enemy lines of communication and supply. Once the retreat across the Pacific had been halted and the Japanese forces held in check, the key to Allied success lay in the control of communications. In the words of General George C. Kenney, Commander of the US Fifth Air Force:

It mattered little whether a Japanese base occupied a small island or a shore-line position on a larger land mass. In either case, there was no effective land line of communications with other bases. For reinforcements or supplies each base was dependent upon sea or air transport, and in the latter category the Japanese never showed the daring and imagination which characterized the American usage. Isolation of any chosen area came to mean then largely an attack on shipping and convoying naval vessels.

As the attacks on enemy communications by carrier aircraft of the US Navy and land-based medium bombers of the 5th Air Force intensified and one Pacific base after another was won back by the Allies, the prospect of bringing the war to the Japanese home islands became more feasible. In the first half of 1944 the Americans possessed an aircraft that would carry out this task — the Boeing B-29 Superfortress — but to reach Japan from a Pacific base even the mighty B-29, with its combat radius of 1,600 miles, would have to wait until the Americans captured Guam and the Mariana group of islands. The time-saving alternative was to strike at Japan from bases in China, from where the B-29S would be able to reach most of Japan's industrial areas. It was also hoped that the presence of the heavy bombers in China would have an advantageous effect on the morale of the Chinese forces, which early in 1944 was giving the American commander in the theatre — Lieutenant-General Joseph S til well — cause for serious concern.

Construction of the B-29 bases in south-west China accordingly went ahead. It was a process beset by considerable difficulties. For a start the only road linking Allied territory with China lay through Burma, and this had been cut by the Japanese advance. All supplies and equipment had therefore to be flown into China from airfields in India or Assam over what was known as the £Hump', an extension of the Himalayas. The transport aircraft made use of a pass, flanked by towering peaks, often battling their way through severe weather, particularly in the monsoon season. As if the climatic problems were not enough, the meagre trickle of supplies that did get through had to be shared between the 20th Air Force, General Claire C. Chennault's 14th Air Force and the Chinese — which led to considerable bickering among the respective commanders, each of whom was inclined to believe that the others were receiving more than their fair slice of the cake. The 20th Bomber Command, as a newly established organization requiring large quantities of bombs, fuel and spare parts, had to fight hard for existence during these early days.

Despite all the difficulties, however, the Command became operational during June 1944, and on the 15th of that month B-29s carried out their first attack on the Japanese mainland. More raids from Chinese territory were carried out during the weeks that followed, but although the 20th's commander, General Curtis LeMay, made superhuman efforts to raise the standard of operational efficiency, the B-29S were able to average only two sorties a month, and some of these were directed against targets in Thailand and Malaya. In all, 20th Bomber Command dropped only 800 tons of bombs on Japanese targets while operating from Chinese bases, and it became increasingly clear that strategic operations against Japan would never be fully effective until bases in the south-west Pacific became available.

On the same day that the B-29S raided Japan for the first time, US Marines went ashore at Saipan in the Marianas, and soon afterwards the islands of Tinian and Guam fell into American hands. The Japanese, however, offered fanatical resistance, which hindered the start of work on bomber bases on Saipan and Tinian, while on Guam Admiral Nimitz decided to use the island as a base for the Pacific Fleet. This meant that all construction work on Guam was under naval control, with the result that the building of airfields came at the very end of the list of priorities.

The first base in the area to be completed was Isley Field, on Saipan, and it was from this location that a B-29 piloted by Captain Ralph D. Steakley flew a reconnaissance mission over Tokyo at 32,000 feet on 1 November 1944, completing the 3,000- mile round trip safely. By a strange coincidence on this same day the Japanese launched their own 'strategic air offensive9 against the United States. This took the shape of 9,000 bomb-carrying paper balloons, which were released from three sites around Tokyo. They were designed to rise to 30,000 feet, where the prevailing westerly winds would, it was hoped, carry them 6,000 miles across the Pacific to the North American continent. Most of the balloons despatched during the months that followed landed harmlessly in the sea or barren areas, but one fell near Lakeview, Oregon, and killed a woman and five of her six children.

The Japanese explosive-balloon campaign was ridiculously puny compared with the vast destruction wrought by the B-29S. During the fourteen months of the American air offensive against Japan, between 15 June 1944 and 15 August 1945, at least 300,000 Japanese citizens were killed and 433,000 injured, while no fewer than 15 million were made homeless.

In January 1945 it was decided to transfer the 20th Bomber Command's two China-based B-29 Wings to the Marianas, where they would form part of the new 20th Air Force under the command of General H. H. Arnold. The 20th Air Force comprised five B-29 Wings, each with an establishment of about 200 bombers, under the operational control of the 21st Bomber Command.

The Command's primary task was the destruction of the Japanese aircraft industry, but because of adverse weather conditions during the winter of 1944-5 and the lack of adequate base facilities, the operational plan got away to a slow start. The B-29 Wings also suffered from a high unserviceability factor, and this -together with the bad weather over Japan-caused many of the raids to be aborted. Much of the blame for the 21st Bomber Command's poor initial record fell somewhat unjustly on its commander, Major-General Haywood S. Hansell, and early in 1945 he was replaced by General Curtis LeMay. At first the latter followed Hansell's policy of carrying out high-level precision attacks on Japanese targets, but achieved no greater success. Nine times out of ten the bomb-aimers found it impossible to pick out their aiming-points through cloud and bad visibility.

Successful radar-directed attacks could, however, be carried out against area targets, and a new directive was accordingly issued to 21st Bomber Command. Although the primary aim was still to be the destruction of the Japanese aircraft and aero-engine industries, 21st Bomber Command was now authorized to carry out large-scale area attacks on selected Japanese cities. If the attacks had to be radar-directed, the chosen cities were Nagoya, Osaka, Kawasaki and Tokyo, in order of priority.

Before this revised plan could be implemented, however, 21st Bomber Command's main effort had to be diverted from strategic operations to tactical support of the American landings on the island of Iwo Jima. The principal reason for invading the island — which could have been by-passed without too much difficulty — was that the Japanese had two major air bases there from which fighters frequently harrassed the B-29S on their way to and from objectives in Japan. Not only would the capture of Iwo remove this thorn in 21st Bomber Command's flesh, but the island's two airstrips would provide valuable emergency landing grounds for Superfortresses in difficulty. They were, in fact, the only alternative to ditching on the long haul over the sea between Japan and the Marianas.

The Americans went ashore on Iwo Jima on 19 February 1945, in the wake of a massive sea and air bombardment. The Japanese garrison resisted fanatically and the Americans had to fight desperately for every square yard of ground: the final cost in human life was 21,304 Japanese and 4,590 Americans killed, with a further 15,954 Americans wounded. Nevertheless there was no denying that the possession of Iwo Jima by the Allies ultimately saved many American lives: before the end of the war more than 2,400 B-29S had made emergency landings on its airfields, and the American air-sea rescue services based on the island saved many bomber crews who were forced to come down in hostile waters.

With Iwo safely in Allied hands, 21st Bomber Command could now go ahead with the area attacks on Japan. After a careful analysis of the problems involved, General LeMay opted in favour of night incendiary attacks. In general there was less cloud over Japan at night and less interference with the bombers' radionavigation aids. Operating under cover of darkness the B-29S could also carry out the raids at lower altitudes, and the reduced need for defensive ammunition meant that heavier bomb loads could be carried.

The first major incendiary attack was launched on the night of 9/10 March 1945, and the target was Tokyo. Shortly after 23.00 the wail of sirens over the Japanese capital heralded the arrival of a small force of B-29 Pathfinder aircraft, which dropped clusters of 70-lb M47 napalm bombs on an aiming point at the centre of a rectangle measuring three miles by four. During the next three hours the Pathfinders were followed by 279 more B-29S, routed individually to the target and stripped of weapons and armour plating to enable them to carry an increased load of 500-lb M69 oil-bomb clusters. Each cluster consisted of sixty 6-lb jellied-oil bombs, released from the main canister at 2,000 feet by a time fuse.

The raid and its catastrophic results were witnessed by Major David H. James, a British Intelligence officer in the prisoner-of-war camp at Omori, just over seven miles south of the Imperial Palace in Tokyo. In his book *The Rise and Fall of the Japanese Empire* he subsequently wrote:

The alert came at 11 pm and soon after the alert the air-raid warnings were being sounded all over Tokyo. About midnight there was the drone of aircraft as the first wave came in from the north-east. They were travelling in two streams — from north-east to south-west and from north to south-east.

Ground defence came into action as the first fires appeared in Oji-ku ... almost at the same time as the leading planes crossed overhead. Planes were flying very low. A strong wind was fanning the fires as wave after wave came over and dropped 'baskets5 of fresh incendiaries over the industrial districts north and east of the Imperial Palace and the factory area to the south-west, bordering Tokyo Bay. Wind direction was north to south. Wave followed wave; they destroyed and then went on into the darkness beyond the flames, their bodies glistening as the beams of searchlights followed them until they were lost to sight in cloud.

The B-29 bomb-aimers in the last waves found their task made difficult by the dense clouds of smoke that billowed over the capital and by the tremendous upcurrents of hot air bursting from the inferno below. There was considerable anti-aircraft fire, although it was generally inaccurate. Nine B-29S were destroyed over the city, and five others were so badly damaged that they had to ditch in the sea; all their crews were picked up safely. Forty-two other bombers sustained varying degrees of flak damage. Seventy-six fighters were sighted and forty attacks were reported, but none of the latter inflicted any damage.

The 1,667 tons of incendiaries dropped by the B-29S caused a glow in the sky that could be seen 150 miles away. The following morning photographs brought back by high-flying B-29 reconnaissance aircraft revealed that 15.8 square miles of Tokyo had been razed to the ground, and that twenty-two major industrial targets had been destroyed. Fire-storms had swept through a quarter of the city's built-up areas, destroying 267,000 buildings and rendering 1,008,000 people homeless. The official Japanese casualty figures gave the number of dead as 83,793, with 102,000 injured; in fact the total was probably far higher. After the war an official told Allied investigators: 'People were unable to escape. They were found later piled upon the bridges, roads and in the canals, 80,000 dead and twice that many injured. We were instructed to report on actual conditions. Most of us were unable to do this because of horrifying conditions beyond imagination.' From his vantage point at Omori, Major James observed the horrific consequences of the raid after daybreak:

All day an acrid smell filled our nostrils ... when the tide lapped our fences it cast up hundreds of charred bodies. We stared through the knot-holes at the men, women and children sprawled in the mud or jammed against the logs from the demolished timber-yards — men, women and children, the remains of human beings left there to rot alongside others who floated in after other raids on the Capital.

The Tokyo raid served to underline the painful inadequacy of the Japanese defences. The early warning system was hopelessly outdated by western standards, and although Tokyo's fire service was the best in Japan it was completely unable to cope with the outbreak of so many large fires over so wide an area. The result was that the inferno became out of hand only half an hour after the start of the raid. The anti-aircraft batteries too — despite the often intense volume of flak they put up — were not radar directed, and consequently most of their fire was wild. The lack of advanced airborne interception radar also severely handicapped the Japanese night-fighter force. The mainstay of the latter was the twin-engined Kawasaki Ki-45 Toryu, known to the Allies by the code-name of 'Nick'. With its armament of one 37-mm and two 20 cannon and one 7.92-mm machine-gun it was a formidable enough opponent, and — had it been equipped with anything but primitive AI — it could have wrought havoc among the B-29 streams. As it was, the day and night defence of Japan came to be borne increasingly by single-engined day-fighter types, and in the latter months of the war the burden of home defence rested almost entirely on the shoulders of the Japanese naval air squadrons.

The ordeal of Japan's cities continued. On the night of 12/13 March it was the turn of Nagoya, the centre of Japan's aircraft industry. Shortly after midnight industrial areas of the city were marked by napalm-carrying B-29 Pathfinders, and during the next three-and-a-half hours 285 bombers unloaded 1,790 tons of incendiaries on and around the aiming points. Nagoya, however, was spared the horrifying catastrophe that had engulfed Tokyo. The city's fire brigade had had the foresight to space firebreaks at key points, the water supply was plentiful, and above all there was only a light wind to fan the flames. On this occasion too the bombers had released their M69 clusters at intervals of 100 feet instead of 50 feet as had been the case in the Tokyo raid, with the result that the incendiaries had been too widely spaced to build up dangerous fire-storms. Nevertheless, although only two square miles of the city had been devastated, eighteen major industrial plants had been destroyed or badly damaged. All the B-29S returned to base; twenty suffered damage, two of them in fighter attacks.

Two nights later the Superfortresses visited Osaka, the second largest city in Japan. Two hundred and seventy-four B-29S made a radar-directed attack on this target through eight-tenths cloud, razing over eight square miles with 1,732 tons of fire bombs. The enemy death toll was 3,988, with a further 9,000 people injured, while 119 factories and 135,000 houses were wiped out. The B-29 crews reported forty attacks by enemy fighters; two bombers failed to return and thirteen more were damaged.

On 17 March 21st Bomber Command's effort was switched against Kobe, a vital enemy port. Once again the attack was radar directed. To achieve a better bombing concentration the aiming points were grouped in a confined area and the duration of the raid was reduced. This time, as supplies of M47 napalm and M69 oil bombs were running low in the Marianas, the B-29S carried M17AIS, magnesium thermite incendiary clusters containing no four-pound bombs. The Kobe raid was the largest to date, with 307 Superfortresses taking part. In the space of just over two hours they dropped 2,355 tons °f incendiaries on the target, totally destroying an area of 2.9 square miles. The Kawasaki shipyards were heavily damaged, while 500 industrial installations were destroyed and 162 damaged. The conflagration destroyed 66,000 houses, making a quarter of a million people homeless; 2,669 were killed and 11,289 injured. Although enemy fighters made ninety-three reported attacks on the raiding force, no B-29S were lost.

On the night of 19/20 March the Superfortresses returned to Nagoya. In addition to a mixed load of M47, M69 and M76 incendiaries, every third carried two 500-lb high-explosive bombs in the hope that these would disrupt the enemy fire services. Two hundred and ninety B-29S dropped a total of 1,858 tons, destroying three square miles of the city. A further raid on Nagoya was carried out on 24 March, this time with 1,500 tons of high explosive. The object of the raid was to carry out a night precision attack on the Mitsubishi aero-engine works, but because of a combination of dense cloud and smoke only sixty tons of bombs actually fell in the target area and the damage inflicted was slight.

The March attacks on Nagoya — in which a total of 820 Superfortresses dropped 5,200 high-explosive and incendiary bombs on the city-were witnessed by an Italian internee, Fosco Maraini, who later described them in his book *Meeting With Japan.*

Each time the warning came at 9 p.m. In the silence, the total darkness of country and town, we could hear the announcements coming from the loudspeakers in the distance: 'Many hundreds of aircraft expected ... Prepare for a heavy raid.' We went down to the shelter with all the bedding we could collect. Towards midnight the air was filled with a powerful throbbing and soon the first waves of B-29S arrived.

They no longer flew at a great height. Every wave dropped a shower of incendiaries, which landed with a sharp crackle, in contrast to the deep roar of high explosive. Meanwhile the city burnt, and the flames rose to the sky. Acres, square miles, of houses and huts, hundreds upon hundreds of tons of timber, blazed in one enormous bonfire, which lasted all night. For us cowering in our shelter the night passed with exasperating slowness. The minutes seemed centuries. When so many aircraft had passed that it seemed no more could be left in the world, as many more approached, flying still lower in the smoky sky, lit up from below by the red glow of the burning town. At last a horrible silence descended, and a ghostly bluish light appeared — the dawn.

For us the worst of these raids was the last [March 24th] when the part of Nagoya where the Tempaku [the house of internment] stood — it was surrounded by suburbs on three sides — was destroyed. The first aircraft bombed one of the quarters immediately to the south; each wave dropped its bombs a little nearer. At one point we thought our turn had come; we held our breath; but the wave passed over without dropping its bombs. The destruction was resumed on the other side of the hills. Several stray bombs fell near us, destroying houses and setting light to stretches of woodland.

At dawn once more we saw the extraordinary bluish light, the first effect of dawn on the night lit up by the orange reflection of fires. The air was laden with smoke, and the horrible smell of burnt flesh [about 10,000 persons lost their lives in these raids].

Beginning on 7 April 1945, 21st Bomber Command turned its major effort to a daylight precision offensive against four of Japan's biggest aero-engine plants: Mitsubishi-Nagoya, Nakajima-Musashi, Mitsubishi-Shizuoka and Hitachi-Yamato. All four were destroyed. On each occasion the Superfortresses were accompanied by P-5 ID Mustang fighters of 7th Fighter Command, based on Iwo Jima — the first land-based Allied fighters to fly over the Japanese home islands.

On the night of 13/14 April the Americans launched another incendiary attack on Tokyo in which 327 B-29S dropped a total of 2,139 tons of incendiaries, wiping out 11.4 square miles of the city. Vast explosions rocked the capital as the fires touched off the contents of munitions factories and arsenals. Two nights later 303 more B-29S bombed Tokyo Bay, Kawasaki and Yokohama, destroying over a quarter of a million buildings.

The strategic bombing campaign against Japan, however, did not proceed without interruption. On 1 April US forces went ashore on Okinawa, the largest of the Ryuku chain of islands lying only 500 miles off the Japanese mainland. By 4 April 60,000 troops had been landed, but although the landings themselves were accomplished with relative ease the Americans soon found themselves involved in what was to become one of the fiercest battles of the war. The Japanese resisted fanatically with every means at their disposal, including swarms of Kamikaze suicide aircraft. In all, 1,900 Kamikaze attacks were made on the Allied fleet off the island. The suicide pilots scored 182 direct hits, sinking twenty-five ships and damaging many more. The situation became so critical that all available air units, including xxi Bomber Command, had to be sent to the assistance of the invasion force. Between 17 April and 11 May more than seventy-five per cent of 21st Bomber Command's total effort was devoted to the tactical offensive against the island's garrison.

While these operations continued a fourth B-29 Wing-the 58th-arrived in the Marianas to join the 73rd, 313th and 314th as part of 21st Bomber Command. On 14 May the Command returned to strategic operations and all four wings put up 472 aircraft for a daylight incendiary attack on Nagoya. The bombers went in at altitudes between 12,000 and 20,000 feet, dropping 2,515 tons of incendiaries on the northern sector of the town, of which 3.2 square miles were destroyed. Many Japanese fighters were in the air and they pressed home determined attacks; 10 B-29s were shot down and 64 were damaged. The B-29 gunners claimed 18 Japanese fighters destroyed.

Nagoya was once again the target on the night of 16/17 May, when 475 B-29S dropped 3,609 tons of incendiaries on the docks area. Each aircraft in the main force carried eight tons of M50 magnesium bombs. The destruction amounted to 3.8 square miles and included one of Mitsubishi's aircraft factories. It was the last time that devastated Nagoya was subjected to an area attack.

On 23 May 21st Bomber Command launched its biggest attack so far. Late in the afternoon 562 Superfortresses took off from the Marianas, arriving over Tokyo shortly after midnight. Attacking through intense flak between 8,000 and 15,000 feet, they unloaded over 3,600 tons of napalm and oil bombs through nine-tenths cloud, smoke and the glare of searchlights, razing 5.3 square miles of the city. Four B-29S were shot down and 69 damaged, all of them by anti-aircraft fire.

Two nights later Tokyo was subjected to its most fearful holocaust yet. A total of 502 aircraft dropped 3,262 tons of incendiaries on the enemy capital; vast firestorms raged through the shattered streets, destroying an area of 16.8 square miles. The Americans, however, did not have things all their own way.

The flak was the heaviest ever encountered by 21st Bomber Command, and the Japanese fighters were up in force; 26 B-29S failed to return and 100 more were damaged, many of them severely.

The Command completed its series of massive incendiary attacks with five raids in daylight against Yokohama, Osaka, Amagasaki and Kobe, carried out between 29 May and 15 June. An average of 450 Superfortresses took part in each mission, dropping a total of 14,132 tons of bombs and destroying an area of 7.9 square miles in Osaka, 6.9 in Yokohama, and 4.4 in Kobe. The raids were not without incident. During the one on Yokohama the bomber formations were heavily attacked by 150 Zero fighters, but these were engaged by the 100 escorting Mustangs and 26 were shot down for the loss of 8 friendly aircraft. A further 175 B-29S were damaged. On 1 June the mission against Osaka was marked by a disaster. The 521 Superfortresses taking part were to have been escorted by 148 P-5 is, but the latter ran into severe thunderstorms and 27 of them collided in mid-air.

Despite tragedies such as these the strategic fire-bombing campaign had enjoyed unqualified success. The official *Army Air Forces in World War II* records:

The six most important industrial cities in Japan had been ruined. Great factories had been destroyed or damaged; thousands of household and feeder industrial units had gone up in smoke. Casualty lists ran into six figures. Millions of persons had lost their homes, and the evacuation of survivors had made it difficult to secure labour for those factories that remained.

21 st Bomber Command was now in a position to concentrate on daylight precision attacks against the enemy aircraft industry, and these were stepped up in June. On the 9th two Bombardment Groups destroyed the Kawanishi airframe factory at Naruo, while two more Groups severely damaged the Aichi engine works at Atsuta. Heavy damage was

also inflicted the following day on the factories of Japan Aircraft at Tomioka, Hitachi Aircraft at Chiba and the 1st Army Air Arsenal at Tachikawa. On the 22nd and 26th it was the turn of the Kawasaki, Kawanishi and Mitsubishi airframe factories, all of which were either wrecked or badly damaged.

On the night of 17/18 June the strategic offensive was switched against Japan's smaller industrial towns. Between that night and the end of the war 21st Bomber Command flew 8,014 sorties against these targets, dropping 54,184 tons of incendiaries. Fifty-seven towns were attacked, thirty-five of them on nine nights in July, when the bombers destroyed a total area of 35.4 square miles. On several days in July the Allied navies took part in the assault, with 2,000 carrier-based aircraft of the US Navy and the British Task Force 57 striking at Tokyo and Hokkaido while Allied battleships turned their heavy guns against steelworks on northern Honshu.

On 24 July, following up the series of carrier strikes, 625 B-29S carried out precision raids on industrial targets in the Nagoya and Osaka areas. A total of 3,539 tons of bombs went down, and all the objectives sustained heavy damage. Some of the targets in fact had already been immobilized before the raids took place, their surviving plant having been shifted elsewhere. In addition to these missions the B-29S laid large quantities of mines around key Japanese ports. They also struck fourteen times at petroleum refineries and synthetic oil plants.

Meanwhile, with the war in Europe at an end, plans were being made for RAF Bomber Command to participate in the final assault on the Japanese homeland. The RAF'S strategic effort in the Far East war had been strictly limited, with the emphasis-because of tactical considerations — being laid on close support. In fact Britain's strategic capability in the Burma-India theatre had been non-existent until 1943, when several squadrons reequipped with the long-range B-24 Liberator. The first B-24 unit to form in India was No. 159 Squadron, which began operations in November 1942. It was joined over the next two years by Nos 160, 355, 356 and 358 Squadrons. Missions flown by the Liberators included supply-dropping, bombing, general reconnaissance, minelaying, anti-submarine work and special duties such as the dropping of agents and supplies to resistance groups.

Now, following the end of the European conflict, the plan called for the transfer of the whole of No. 5 Group, Bomber Command, to the Pacific theatre under the code-name of 'Tiger Force'. It was to operate from an island close to Okinawa, some 200 miles east of the northern tip of Formosa and 1,150 miles south-west of Tokyo. The force was to be equipped with either the Lancaster or Avro's longer-range version the Lincoln, with Mosquitoes as pathfinders. If everything went to schedule the first eight squadrons of Tiger Force were to be operational by 1 December, and more squadrons were to be added at the rate of four a month until the force reached its planned strength of twenty squadrons. At the nucleus of Tiger Force were to be Nos 9 and 617 Squadrons, which were to use Tallboy and Grand Slam bombs against Japanese precision targets. Operational plans were drawn up by 1 June 1945 and the squadrons involved began intensive training, while Bomber Command observers — including Group Captain Cheshire — were sent out to the Far East to liaise with their American counterparts.

Tiger Force, however, was destined never to see combat. In the Far East events were moving towards their dramatic climax. On 1 August 1945 21 st Bomber Command carried out devastating fire raids on four small cities in northern and central Honshu. The largest of them, Toyama, was completely destroyed, while ninety per cent of Hachioji was razed. On the night of 5/6 August the B-29S once again visited the cities of Honshu, causing devastation which, in a matter of hours, was to be overshadowed by an even grimmer spectacle of destructive power.

At 08.15 hours on Monday, 6 August a single B-29 with the name 'Enola Gay5 emblazoned on its side droned high over the city of Hiroshima, in southern Honshu. From its belly fell the first operational atomic bomb, nicknamed 'Little Boy5. Minutes later 4.7 square miles of Hiroshima lay totally destroyed beneath the ascending mushroom cloud. In all, 70,000 people died and as many more were injured by blast, heat and radiation. The next day President Truman announced to the world: 'Sixteen hours ago an American airplane dropped one bomb on Hiroshima, an important Japanese Army base. That bomb had more power than 20,000 tons of TNT ... It is an atomic bomb.'

Despite the tremendous impact caused by the destruction of Hiroshima conventional air attacks continued. On 7 August 131 B-29S attacked the big naval base at Tokokawa, and the next day 221 Superfortresses, escorted by p-47 Thunderbolts, struck at the massive enemy steelworks at Yawata, on north-western Kyushu. That same night the port of Fukuyama was the target of an incendiary attack that destroyed three-quarters of its built-up areas.

On the morning of Thursday, 9 August another lone B-29 dropped the second atomic bomb on Nagasaki. For geographical reasons — primarily because the aiming point was sheltered by surrounding hills — the loss of life at Nagasaki was much less than had been the case at Hiroshima. Nevertheless this second nuclear attack — together with the invasion of Japanese-held Manchuria by the Soviet Union that same day-pushed the Japanese Government over the brink to unconditional surrender.

And still, in those last days, the massed formations of B-29S roved over the sky of Japan. On 14 August 449 Superfortresses, escorted by 186 Mustangs and Thunderbolts, struck at the last remaining targets — the naval arsenal at Hikari, the Osaka Army Arsenal, the Marifu marshalling yards near Hiroshima and the Nippon Oil Co. plant at Atika. That night the B-29S carried out a heavy incendiary raid on Kumagaya and Isezaki, north-west of Tokyo.

Even before this raid took place Japan had decided to accept the Allies5 unconditional surrender terms. The last hours were described by Saburo Sakai, Japan's leading fighter ace, in his book *Samurai*.

Japan was about to *surrender*.

'Sakai.' I looked up. 'Saburo, it ... it is just about the end now.' Kawachi spoke. 'We have very little time left. Let us make one more flight together, one last flight.' He kicked the ground idly with his foot. 'We just can't quit like this,' he protested. 'We have to draw blood once more.'

I nodded. He was right. We told the maintenance men to move our two Zeros out to the runway, to prepare them for flight. We knew that the Superfortresses would bomb tonight. The weather forecast appeared promising, and there were so many bombers overhead every evening that B-29S could be intercepted almost anywhere. For a long time they had flown over Oppama without opposition, using the field for a landmark. They would not expect fighters.

Kawachi and I kept our plans strictly to ourselves, not even telling the other pilots ... The afternoon passed and we remained seated, almost invisible in the darkness. Shortly before midnight the tower radio spluttered. 'Alert. Alert. A B-29 formation is now approaching the Yokosuka-Tokyo area.'

We jumped to our feet and ran across the field to our planes. The air base lay in blackness, not a light showing. There was just enough light from the stars to enable us to make our way. When we reached the Zeros, we discovered we were not the only pilots determined to go up for a last mission. At least eight other fighters were lined up at the edge of the runway, fuelled and armed.

The moment we were airborne, I swung in close to Kawachi's fighter and took up a position off his wing. Eight other Zeros were in the air with us, forming into two flights behind our planes. We climbed steadily, then circled at 10,000 feet over Tokyo Bay.

Kawachi's fighter banked abruptly and pulled away to the east. I flew with him, the two flights close behind. For a few moments I failed to see any other planes in the air. Then Kawachi's cannon started firing, and I made out the big bomber flying northward. I had him now, clear in my sights. I pulled up almost alongside Kawachi's plane and opened fire. We each had four cannon now, and we would need every weapon against the tremendous airplane. I had never seen anything so huge! As I swung around after completing my firing pass, I saw the eight other fighters storming the Superfortress. They appeared like tiny gnats milling round a tremendous bull. How could we hope to shoot down an airplane of such incredible size?

I came in again, climbing and sending my fire into the B-29S underside. The counterfire was terrible. Tracers spilled into the air from the multiple turrets of the B-29, and I felt the Zero shudder several times as the enemy gunners found their mark. We ignored the bomber guns and kept pressing home the attack. The Superfortress turned and headed south. Apparently we had damaged the big plane, and now he was running for home. I clung to Kawachi and slammed the engine on overboost. The other eight fighters were already lost far behind us, and it was doubtful that we could keep up with the bomber. It possessed remarkable speed and was, in fact, faster than the Zeros I had flown at Lae.

Kawachi, however, had no intention of losing the big plane in the dark. He cut inside the B-2g's wide turn and led me down in a shallow diving attack. This time we had a clear shot, and both Kawachi and I kept the *triggers down, watching the tracers and shells ripping into the glass along the bomber's nose. We had him! Suddenly, the Superfortress's speed fell off and the pilot dropped the airplane down for a long dive. We came around in a tight turn, firing steadily in short bursts, pouring the cannon shells into the crippled plane.*

The great bomber descended quickly. I saw no fire or smoke. There was no visible damage, but the airplane continued to lose altitude steadily, dropping towards the ocean. We kept after the fleeing plane. O Shima Island suddenly loomed up out of the darkness. We were fifty miles south of Yokosuka.

We pulled out of our dives, and climbed to 1,500 feet. A volcano on the island reared 1,000 feet above the water, and we dared not risk a collision in the blackness. I could make out the bomber faintly as it dropped. Presently it ditched with a splash of white foam in the ocean, several miles off O Shima's southern coastline. In less than a minute the B-29 disappeared beneath the water.

Back at the airfield, we learned that at least three cities had been gutted during the night. The fires were still burning fiercely, unchecked, sweeping before the wind.

The war was to end less than twelve hours later ...

In the final analysis it was the B-29 that destroyed Japan's capacity for waging war. Although there is no doubt that it was the atomic bomb that brought Japan to the surrender table, it was only the last of a long series of shattering blows. Japan had been seriously weakened by the terrible losses she had sustained both in the Pacific and Burma, and she was being slowly strangled by the Allied blockade of her communications. Nevertheless it was the continual battering by the B-29S of 21st Bomber Command, more than any other single cause, that brought her to defeat. The great fire raids on sixty of Japan's cities had a fearful effect on civilian morale, and the dispersal of her aircraft and aero-engine plants under conditions of panic caused as much dislocation of production as did the raids themselves. In the words of the Japanese Premier, Suzuki:

It seemed to me unavoidable that in the long run Japan would be almost destroyed by air attack, so that merely on the basis of the B-29S alone I was convinced that Japan should sue for peace. On top of the B-29S raids came the atomic bombs, after the Potsdam Declaration, which was just one additional reason for giving in. I myself, on the basis of the B-29 raids, felt that the cause was hopeless.

At no other time in the history of air warfare had the strategic bomber succeeded so overwhelmingly in its task.

Appendix 1: Chronology of Principal Allied Strategic Bombing Operations 1945-5

1943 Jan:

1 - No. 6 (Royal Canadian Air Force) Group assumes operational status with eight squadrons at 00.01 hours.

8 - Bomber Command's Pathfinder Force re-designated No. 8 Group (PFF).

16/17 - Lancasters of No. 5 Group attack Berlin and make first operational use of 250-lb target indicator bombs.

21 - The Casablanca Directive, defining Allied bombing policy, issued by the Combined Chiefs of Staff.

27 - First USAAF raid on Germany; bombers of the US 8th Air Force attack Wilhelmshaven in daylight.

30 - First RAF daylight attack on Berlin by Mosquitoes of Nos 105 and 139 Squadrons.

30/31 - First operational use of H2S radar by Stirlings and Halifaxes of Nos 7 and 35 PFF Squadrons, leading main force in an attack on Hamburg

Feb:

4 – US 8th Air Force B-I 7s attack Emden; six aircraft fail to return.

16 - Eight B-17s lost during attack on St Nazaire.

17 - Allied Command in Mediterranean reorganized. Establishment of Mediterranean Air Command under Air Chief Marshal Sir Arthur Tedder, who is responsible for all air operations in north-west Africa.

22 - First operational use of North American Mitchells of RAF Bomber Command: Nos 98 and 180 Squadrons attack oil installations at Terneuzen.

25 - Start of the Allied 'round the clock' bombing offensive. During the next 48 hours the Allied Air Forces fly more than 2,000 sorties against enemy targets.

26 - Establishment of the North-West African Air Forces under General Carl Spaatz. It comprises the North-West African Strategic Air Force under General J. H. Doolittle, with two US bombardment wings

and No. 205 Group RAF, together with the North-West African Tactical Air Force under Air Marshal Sir A. Coningham.

Mar:

5/6 - Bomber Command's 'Battle of the Ruhr' begins with an attack by 345 aircraft on Essen. 'Oboe' used on a large scale for the first time. 14 bombers fail to return and 32 are damaged.

8 – US 8th Air Force bombers begin a series of heavy attacks on marshalling yards and other rail targets in enemy territory.

18 - 73 B-17S and 24 B-24S attack the Vulcan shipbuilding yards at Vegesack in the biggest single mission carried out by the 8th Bomber Command to date.

Apr:

4 - 85 B-17S drop 251 tons of high explosive on the Renault factory in the suburbs of Paris while aircraft of No. 2 Group RAF carry out diversionary attacks elsewhere. Target severely damaged; four bombers fail to return.

17 - 115 B-17S despatched to attack the Focke-Wulf factories at Bremen. 16 bombers FTR.

May:

14 - First large-scale attack by US 8th Air Force on several different targets simultaneously, with 200 Fortresses and Liberators despatched to attack Ijmuiden, Gourtrai, Antwerp and Kiel. 11 aircraft, mostly Liberators, FTR.

16/17 - Mohne and Eder dams attacked and breached by Lancasters of No. 617 Squadron RAF, led by Wing Commander Guy Gibson, who is subsequently awarded the VC. A third dam, the Sorpe, also damaged in the raid.

June:

10 - Directive for 'Operation Pointblank' — the combined bombing offensive by Bomber Command and the US 8th Air Force — issued by the Combined Chiefs of Staff.

11 - The island of Pantellaria occupied by Allied forces following a concentrated air bombardment lasting 20 days — the first time a heavily defended objective of such a size has been completely overwhelmed by air power.

20/21 - First 'shuttle-bombing' operation by RAF Bomber Command; bomber force lands at Algiers after attacking Friedrichshafen and raids Spezia on the return flight to the UK three nights later.

July:

9/10 - Large-scale Allied bombing offensive supports landings in Sicily (Operation Husky).

24/25 - Bomber Command carries out the first of four large-scale attacks on Hamburg (Operation Gomorrah) using 'Window' for the first time. Series of attacks ends on the night of 2/3 August.

24: US 8th Air Force begins 'Big Week' air offensive with an attack on Trondheim, followed by a raid on the Blohm & Voss shipyards at Hamburg the next day.

26 - B-17S attack the Continental Gummiwerke AG at Hanover. 16 bombers fail to return, with a further 8 destroyed over Hamburg and other secondary targets.

27 - USAAF begins a three-day series of strikes against German aircraft factories, carrying out five major raids on sixteen different targets. During the 'Big Week' offensive the 8th Bomber Command loses 88 aircraft, mostly B-17S.

Aug:

1 - Five Bombardment Groups — 177 aircraft-of the US gth Air Force despatched from North Africa to attack oil refineries at Ploesti in Rumania. 50 B-24 Liberators fail to return.

17 - 376 B-I 7s of US 8th Air Force despatched to attack ballbearing factories at Schweinfurt and Regensburg. Bombers encounter intense opposition, including air-to-air rocket attacks, and 60 fail to return.

17/18 - Bomber Command despatches 597 heavy bombers in first attack on German rocket research centre at Peenemunde. 40 aircraft FTR.

31 - Enemy night-fighter force makes first large-scale use of 'Wilde Sau' tactics, with night-fighters dropping flares over bomber stream and making individual attacks.

Sep:

15/16 - First operational use of 12,000-lb Tallboy bombs by Lancasters of No. 617 Squadron in low-level attack on the Dortmund-Ems Canal. 5 aircraft out of 8 despatched FTR; 2 bombed the primary target.

22/23 - Bomber Command employs 'Spoof' tactics for the first time, with main force attacking Hanover while electronic countermeasures aircraft simulate raid against Oldenburg.

1944 January:

20 - Strategic Air Forces launch the biggest air onslaught in history against key aircraft factories between Leipzig and Brunswick, with 941 bombers and 700 fighters taking part. 21 bombers FTR. Daylight raids followed up that night by a raid by 600 Lancasters and Halifaxes of Bomber Command on Stuttgart.

22 - Liberators and Fortresses of the 15th Air Force attack Regensburg while the 8th Air Force strikes at targets in central Germany.

24 - 600 heavy bombers of the 8th and 15th Air Forces attack Schweinfurt, Styria, Gotha and other aeroengine and airframe plants. Schweinfurt again attacked after dark by 700 aircraft of RAF Bomber Command.

25 – US Strategic Air Forces launch massive raid with 800 bombers on the Messerschmitt factories at Regensburg and Augsburg 64 aircraft FTR.

Mar:

6 USAAF strikes for the first time at Berlin with 660 bombers. 69 aircraft FTR. Forty-eight hours later, another raid on the German capital by 580 bombers and 801 fighters costs the Americans 54 aircraft.

15 - Allied Air Forces drop 1,100 tons of bombs on Cassino.

30/31 - Bomber Command suffers its heaviest loss of the war in one raid: out of 795 Lancasters and Halifaxes despatched to Nuremberg, 95 FTR.

April:

British and American bombers carry out a series of 24 attacks by day and night on the enemy oil refineries at Ploesti, in Rumania.

11 - Six Mosquitoes of No. 613 Squadron attack Gestapo HQ, in The Hague.

14 - Strategic bombing in the European theatre placed under the control of the Supreme Commander Allied Expeditionary Force, General Eisenhower, in preparation for the Allied invasion.

May:

12 - Strategic bombing emphasis switches from attacks on enemy aircraft industry to oil installations. 935 heavy bombers and 1,000

fighters strike at five major synthetic oil plants, destroying or severely damaging all of them.

June:

2 - USAAF begins shuttle-bombing operations between Italy and Russia. B-17S of the 15th Air Force take off from Italian bases, attack Debrecen airfield in Hungary and land at Poltava in the Ukraine.

5/6 - Bomber Command carries out extensive tactical operations in support of the Allied landings in Normandy. Operations include attacks on heavy coastal gun batteries, radio countermeasures and the simulation of airborne landings with the aid of dummy paratroops. Massive support by all Allied strategic and tactical air forces continues throughout the landing phase.

8/9 - First operational use of strengthened deep-penetration variant of 12,000-lb Tallboy bomb; 19 dropped by Lancasters of 617 Squadron in successful raid on the Saumur railway tunnel. Before the end of hostilities Bomber Command drops a total of 854 Tallboys on enemy targets.

15 - First American air attack on the Japanese mainland by land-based aircraft: B-29 Superfortresses of the 20th Air Force, operating from bases in sw China.

16/17 - Beginning of intensive period of attacks by Bomber Command on V-I flying bomb sites on the French coast, lasting until 6 September.

July:

18 - Bomber Command drops over 5,000 tons of bombs in support of the 21st Army Group's offensive SE of Caen.

Aug:

14/15: Allied strategic air forces operate intensively in support of Operation Dragoon, the Allied invasion of southern France.

27: First major daylight operation against a German target in 1944: 216 Halifaxes of 4 Group and 27 Mosquitoes and Lancasters of 5 Group, accompanied by strong Spitfire escort, attack oil installations at Homburg in the Ruhr. First penetration by Bomber Command east of the Rhine with fighter cover.

Sep:

8: Last operational bombing mission by Stirlings of Bomber Command: an attack on Le Havre by 149 Squadron.

23/24: Dortmund-Ems Canal breached by Lancasters of No. 5 Group Bomber Command.

Oct:

3 - Large daylight attack by Bomber Command results in breaching of a dyke near Westkapelle on Walcheren Island.

7 - Kembs Dam on the Upper Rhine breached by Lancasters of 617 Squadron to prevent the Germans from releasing flood waters to impede the Allied advance.

14/15 - Largest number of sorties ever despatched by Bomber Command in one night — 1,576. A total of 1,294 tons of bombs dropped on German targets.

Nov:

4/5 - Dortmund-Ems Canal attacked and breached again by Lancasters of No. 5 Group.

12 - German battleship *Tirpitz* sunk by Lancasters of Nos 9 and 617 Squadrons in Tromso Fjord, using 12,000-lb bombs.

16 - Both Bomber Command and US 8th Air Force give close support to offensive by American ground forces towards Cologne. Largest number of sorties despatched by Bomber Command in one day — 1,189 on all operations. Also greatest tonnage of bombs dropped – 5,689.

21/22 - Dortmund-Ems Canal and Mitteland Canal both breached by Lancasters of No. 5 Group.

Dec:

16 - Start of intensive period of air operations by Allied bombing forces against German offensive in the Ardennes.

31 - Gestapo HQ, at Oslo attacked by Mosquitoes of No. 627 Squadron Bomber Command.

1945 Jan:

1 - Dortmund-Ems Canal once again attacked and breached by aircraft of No. 5 Group, followed by the Mitteland Canal the next night.

Feb 20/21 - Mosquitoes of RAF Bomber Command carry out the first of 36 consecutive nightly raids on Berlin, ending on 27/28 March.

March 9/10 - 279 B-29S of US 20th Air Force carry out devastating fire raid on Tokyo, dropping 1,667 tons of incendiaries and killing over 80,000 people.

11 - Heaviest tonnage of bombs dropped on one target in a single day: 4,661 tons on Essen by 1,055 Lancasters, Halifaxes and Mosquitoes of Bomber Command. Raid carried out through 10/10 cloud.

12 - Previous day's record exceeded by 1,079 Lancasters, Halifaxes and Mosquitoes of Bomber Command, dropping 4,851 tons of bombs on Dortmund. Largest number of aircraft despatched by RAF against one target in a single day.

12/13 - 285 B-29S drop 1,790 tons of incendiaries on Nagoya.

14 - First operational use of 22,000-lb Grand Slam bomb by the RAF; dropped on the Bielefeld Viaduct by Lancaster 1 PDI12 of No. 617 Squadron, flown by Squadron Leader G. C. Calder. Forty more Grand Slams dropped on enemy targets before the end of hostilities.

14/15 - 274 B-29S carry out incendiary attack on Osaka, second city of Japan.

17 - 307 B-29S of xxi Bomber Command make radar-directed daylight attack on Kobe, dropping 2,355 tons of incendiaries.

19/20 - 290 Superfortresses drop 1,858 tons of incendiaries on Nagoya, destroying three square miles of the city.

21 - Successful attack on Gestapo HQ, at Copenhagen by Mosquitoes of Nos 21, 464 and 487 Squadrons.

24 - Allied strategic air forces support crossing of the Rhine (Operation Varsity).

24 - Daylight attack on Nagoya by xxi Bomber Command; 1,500 tons of high explosive dropped.

27 - Lancasters of Nos 9 and 617 Squadrons destroy u-Boat pens at Farge using Tallboys and Grand Slams.

Apr 9/10 - German pocket battleship *Admiral Scheer* capsized and cruisers *Emden* and *Hipper* badly damaged during attack on Kiel by Bomber Command.

13/14 - Second large incendiary attack on Tokyo; 327 B-29S drop 2,139 tons on the city.

17 - Objectives of 'Operation Pointblank' achieved.

25 - Six Mosquitoes of Nos 21, 464 and 487 Squadrons carry out successful attack on Gestapo HQ at Odense. 318 Lancasters of Nos 1, 5 and 8 Groups attack Hitler's mountain chalet and the ss barracks at Berchtesgaden in support of offensive by the US 7th Army, while 468

Lancasters, Halifaxes and Mosquitoes of Nos 4, 6, 8 and 100 Groups attack coastal gun batteries on the island of Wangerooge.

25/26 - 92 Lancasters and 8 Mosquitoes attack oil refinery at Vallo — the last raid by main-force heavy bombers of the RAF on an enemy target in the Second World War. Twelve Lancasters of No. 5 Group also carry out the RAF'S last minelaying operation, in Oslo Fjord.

26 - Allied Air Forces begin Operation Exodus — the repatriation of prisoners of war. Operation continues until 1 June, by which time Bomber Command alone flies home 75,000 POWS.

May 2/3 - Last offensive action by RAF Bomber Command in the Second World War. 303 sorties flown by Mosquitoes of No. 8 Group against enemy airfields, while aircraft of No. 100 Group fly bomber support missions.

8 - Unconditional surrender of Germany.

14 - 472 Superfortresses carry out daylight incendiary attack on Nagoya.

16/17 - 475 B-29S drop 3,609 tons of incendiaries on harbour area of Nagoya.

23 - XXI Bomber Command launches biggest raid so far on Japan; 562 B-29S drop 3,600 tons of incendiaries on Tokyo.

25/26 - Heaviest raid on Tokyo so far; 502 B-29S drop 3,262 tons of incendiaries, destroying 16.8 square miles of the city. 26 B-29S FTR.

June - Between 29 May and 15 June, xxi Bomber Command carries out five major daylight raids on Yokohama, Osaka, Kobe and Amagasaki, dropping 14,132 tons of bombs.

17/18 - XXI Bomber Command's strategic offensive switched to Japan's smaller industrial towns. Up to the end of the war the Command carries out 8,014 sorties against these targets and drops 54,184 tons of bombs in attacks on 57 towns.

July 24 - 625 B-29S carry out a series of precision attacks on industrial targets in the Nagoya and Osaka areas, dropping 3,529 tons of bombs. Superfortresses also lay mines off key Japanese ports and strike at Japanese oil refineries.

Aug 6 - Atomic bomb dropped on Hiroshima.

7 - 131 B-29S attack naval base at Tokokawa.

8 - 221 B-29S escorted by Thunderbolts hit enemy steelworks at Yawata, followed by incendiary attack on Fukuyama.

9 - Second atomic bomb dropped on Nagasaki.

14 - 449 Superfortresses carry out attacks on naval arsenal at Hikari, Osaka Army Arsenal, Marifu marshalling yards at Hiroshima and Nippon Oil Co. plant at Atika.

14/15 - B-29S carry out heavy incendiary attack on Kumagaya and Isezaki — the last strategic mission undertaken by xxi Bomber Command in the Second World War.

15 - Unconditional surrender of Japan.

Appendix 2 – Glossary

Airborne Cigar: Radio countermeasures device for jamming enemy VHF communications between ground stations and fighters.

Crossbow, Operation: Allied offensive against enemy v-weapon sites.

Gee: Fixing system relaying electronic pulses from three ground stations to receiver equipment in aircraft. The latter measures difference in time of receipt of signals from ground stations and converts the resulting information into terms of distance. Two sets of readings are plotted on a special chart known as a Gee Lattice Chart; the point of intersection is the enemy's position.

G-H: Highly accurate blind-bombing system in which the aircraft transmits pulse signals to two ground stations, which receive the pulses and transmit them back. This enables the aircraft to measure continuously its distance from two known points, track itself over any target within range of the system and determine its bomb-release point.

Grand Slam: 22,000-pound deep-penetration bomb.

H2S: Radio aid to navigation, target location and bombing, which transmits pulse signals to earth and receives back the echoes, which form a display on a cathode-ray tube. This display consists of a series of light spots of varying brilliance, which form a picture of the terrain over which the aircraft is flying.

Johnny Walker: Anti-shipping bomb similar in configuration to, but smaller than, the mine used in the raid on the Ruhr dams.

Mandrel: Airborne radio countermeasures 'screen' designed to jam enemy early warning radar.

Naxos: Enemy night-fighter radar enabling fighters to home on to H2S transmissions.

Newhaven: Method of marking a target by flares or TIS dropped blindly on H2S indications.

Oboe: Radio aid to bombing in which two ground stations transmit pulses to an aircraft, which then receives them and retransmits them. By measuring the time taken for each pulse to go out and return, the distance of the aircraft from the ground stations can be accurately measured. If the distance of the target from Station A is known, the aircraft can be guided along the arc of a circle whose radius equals this distance. The bomb-release point is calculated and determined by Station B, which instructs' the aircraft to release its bomb load when the objective is reached.

Overlord: The Allied invasion of France, June 1944.

Pointblank: Directive for the combined Allied bombing offensive against Germany, June 1943.

Serrate: Radar countermeasures device enabling night-fighters to home on to the radar transmissions of enemy aircraft.

Tallboy: 12,000-pound bomb.

Window: Strips of tinfoil, cut to the wavelength of enemy warning radar and dropped in bundles from attacking aircraft to confuse enemy defences.

37313272R00094

Printed in Poland
by Amazon Fulfillment
Poland Sp. z o.o., Wrocław